Mystery Tour

By the same author:

KICK START
SKIN FOR SKIN
BLACK LEATHER MURDERS
THE CREEPING FLESH

Mystery Tour

Douglas Rutherford

WALKER AND COMPANY
New York

First published in the United States of America in 1976 by the Walker Publishing Company, Inc.

ISBN: 0-8027-5356-6

Library of Congress Catalog Card Number: 76-24562

Printed in the United States of America.

10 9 8 7 6 5 4 3 2 1

CONNOISSEUR TOURS

CITIES AND LAKES OF ITALY

Passenger List

Name	*Residence*
Benson Mr R. T.	Hastings
Collins Mr J.	Croydon
Collins Mrs	,,
Forsythe Mr E. K.	London
Foxell Miss Amelia	Bury St Edmunds
Grant Mr Frederick	Chelmsford
Grant Mrs	,,
Hayward Mrs G. St C.	Tonbridge
Jones Mr Gareth	Newtown (Montgomeryshire)
Jones Mrs	,,
Meredith Mrs Diana	Bath
Norman Miss Alice	London
Preston Mr B. G.	Warminster
Preston Mrs	,,
Preston Miss Emma	,,
Preston Master Nigel	,,
Rayburn Mrs Lucy	Liverpool
Sloman Mrs	Tonbridge
Tasker Mr Alan	Newcastle-upon-Tyne
Wilkins Miss Doreen	London

CHAPTER I

'BEFORE you say any more, sir, I have to caution you – '

'*What?*'

Ken's head jerked up in total amazement. The detective-sergeant's rugged features had become cold and formal, as if he were trying to master a sense of acute distaste – even revulsion.

'I am arresting you on suspicion of murder. You will be taken to the police station and charged,' Detective-Sergeant Spurling stated with formal clarity. 'You are not obliged to say anything unless you wish to do so, but whatever you say will be taken down in writing and may be used in evidence.'

The officially approved formula had been recited like a well-learned lesson. Ken shook his head, not in denial so much as bewilderment. He looked round the small room for some evidence that he was not in the grip of a nightmare. His eyes found a corner table on which reposed a leather case. It was a portable kit containing all that is needed to administer the Last Rites to the dying – ritual book, purple stole and oil stock. The chaplain's office, tucked away in the basement of Gatwick Airport, was shared by both the Protestant and Roman Catholic priests.

Just behind him a pair of shoes creaked. Young Detective-Constable Carter had recently been transferred to the CID and this was his first experience of arresting a murderer. A double murderer too.

'What is the charge going to be?'

'You will be charged at the station.'

'I have a right to know who I'm supposed to have murdered.'

Spurling hesitated. He was sensitive about a suspect's rights, having once lost a cut-and-dried case because of a technicality over the method of arrest and interrogation.

He was confident that he was not obliged to do more than caution the man at this stage. But the suspect had been thrown badly off balance by the caution. There was a chance that he might say something incriminating. If so, that was his funeral. He'd had his warning.

'You will be charged with the murder of Mr Tony Draper at the Crown Hotel on the night of 21st April and of Mrs Lucy Rayburn in this room on the evening of the 22nd.'

The room rocked before Ken's incredulous eyes.

'Why on earth would I have wanted to kill Mrs Rayburn? I mean, all I knew was that she'd missed the plane.'

'She missed it because her body had been locked inside that cupboard.' Spurling nodded towards the steel locker where the priests kept their vestments for Sunday services.

'And the murder at the Crown Hotel in Earl's Court. Wasn't that the work of some sadistic sex maniac? You're making a colossal mistake, Inspector –'

'Detective-Sergeant.'

'Okay, but you're still on the wrong track. I can prove –'

'You can tell us all that when we take your statement, sir.' Spurling's unemotional voice cut in on Ken's impulsive comment. He glanced up and the two detectives exchanged some unspoken message. Carter would be able to state under oath that the suspect had been properly cautioned.

Ken stared at the suitcase on the table in front of him and the pile of incriminating contents which lay beside it. A sexual pervert's armoury. His mind was racing, tracking back over the events of the past week.

'Listen,' he said urgently. 'I can see why you're arresting me, but you're making a mistake. The real murderer is back there in Italy – at Castelvecchio. I know who it is now and I'm certain that he's going to kill again. I've got to get back and warn her – I mean them. The Italian police inspector –'

He stopped, conscious that the man behind him was rapidly noting down every word he spoke.

'As a matter of fact,' Spurling said evenly, 'we are already in touch with the Italian authorities. But if you wish to make a statement here it must be taken down in writing.'

Ken remained silent for a long minute. Spurling waited. He hoped now that his man would agree to making a proper written statement. This was the most likely moment to obtain a confession, when the suspect was still reeling from the impact of the arrest. He felt he had won the advantage and he intended to exploit it.

Ken had little doubt that he could prove his innocence in the long run, despite the fact that he had been caught red-handed with the suitcase and its obscene contents. But once at the police station he would become trapped in the deliberately slow and formalized procedures of the judicial system. They might hold him for days and meanwhile . . .

'I want to make a statement now.'

'You wish to make a statement here?'

'Yes.' Ken nodded decisively. He had made up his mind. 'I do. Will you write it or do I?'

'Either way. I can write it for you, if you wish.'

Spurling concealed his satisfaction as he reached for his brief-case. This way he could take the statement down in a correct form which would stand up to examination in court. Spurling, like every experienced CID officer, was well versed in the Judges' Rules, and he had no intention of letting this fish get off the hook just because some smart defence counsel found a fault in his arrest procedure.

The man appeared to have been shocked into a state of docile co-operation. It was usually the case with these sex killers. On an earlier assignment he had tracked down the perpetrator of a crime of horrifying bestiality and violence only to find a meek little family man who looked incapable of swatting a mosquito. He had to admit, though, that this chap was a different matter. He was tall, sun-tanned, lean and fit. He shouldn't have any trouble finding women ready and willing to satisfy his passions, but that was evidently not enough for him. CID work was full of surprises.

'If you'd sit there, sir, at the opposite side of the table.'

Ken noticed that, even now when the contents of the suitcase had been exposed, he did not drop the 'sir'. Spurling's revulsion had shown only briefly on his chunky features when the tray masking the bottom of the case had been lifted out.

Ken sat at the place indicated. Detective-Constable Carter moved quietly till he was standing just behind the upright metal chair. Spurling smoothed the charge form he had extracted from his brief-case and took the Biro from his breast pocket.

'Your full name, please.'

'Edward Kenneth Forsythe.'

'Is that spelt with a "y", sir?'

'Yes.' Ken spoke wearily. 'And there's an "e" on the end.'

Spurling wrote deliberately for a few moments in his careful, neat hand. Ken felt that familiar weakness and trembling in his limbs which preceded explosive action. He'd known it ever since he could remember – before a boxing-match at school, waiting to take the baton in a relay race, building up revolutions on the starting line before a timed section in the RAC rally. He was finding it an effort to sustain the pose of slumped despair and resignation.

Spurling meticulously inscribed a last word and added three dots. He twisted the sheet round and pushed it towards Ken.

He had written : 'I Edward Kenneth FORSYTHE wish to make a statement. I want someone to write down what I say. I have been told that I need not say anything and that whatever I say may be given in evidence.

Signed . . .'

'Is all this necessary?'

'Yes. It's required by the Judges' Rules.'

Ken murmured : 'A man is helping the police with their enquiries.'

The sound of a jet taking off and gaining height penetrated faintly to this underground room. From beyond the door came a chatter of voices as a party descended the moving staircase to the bus station.

Ken accepted the offer of a pen, pushed his chair back a foot and signed the preamble. With a gesture of hopeless resignation he pushed the paper back to the other man.

'My pen, I think.'

'Oh yes. Sorry.'

Ken threw the pen chest high so that the other had to put his hands up and take it like a catch at slip. At the same instant Ken lifted one foot, slammed it against the edge of the table and shoved with all his strength. Projected forward, the edge of the table caught Spurling in the stomach. His chair rocked and he fell backwards to the floor. Ken's own chair had been driven by the thrust of his leg against the lower part of DC Carter's body. He twisted as he fell, jabbed an elbow viciously against the detective's jaw. Scrambling up, he saw that Spurling was getting on to one knee. He put his hands under the table and heaved it away from him. The suitcase, its contents and a mass of papers cascaded on top of the CID man. The edge of the table thumped his throat.

As Ken made for the door, Carter reached out to grab his leg. Ken spun and kicked him hard in the diaphragm. He did not wait to observe the result. He could hear Carter choking as he removed the key from the lock on the inside. He went out rapidly, closed the door, locked it, put the key in his pocket.

He walked at a brisk pace towards the moving staircase. Half a dozen passengers, members of some student travel group, were standing on it, their suitcases and kit-bags cluttering the steps. Ken went up the fixed middle staircase, taking the steps three at a time. From the door of the chaplain's office came the sound of furious banging and muffled shouts of: 'Stop that man! Stop him!'

A couple whom Ken was passing glanced at him with detached curiosity. He grinned at them and they smiled back.

Crossing the shiny floor of the Main Hall of Gatwick Airport he resisted the temptation to run. The main entrance was twenty seconds away. He felt sure the place must be crawling with plainclothes detectives. It would be extraordinary if the police had left only two men to spring their trap. Everything depended on how quickly the airport exchange answered the call which Spurling or Carter must surely be making.

A score of passengers sitting in the waiting area were laughing at the antics of a small boy of four who was trying to propel one of the hefty luggage trolleys. Ken had to swerve to avoid him.

He pushed through the swing-doors to the pavement, brushing past the uniformed police constable, who was glaring warningly at any driver who showed signs of leaving his car there. The Rover V8 was parked on the double yellow lines, just under the notice which stated that vehicles could only stop here to pick up or set down passengers. The traffic warden, standing level with the windscreen, was preparing to make out a parking ticket.

At least that gave Ken an excuse to run. As the warden saw him coming he smiled ruefully and put his pad away.

'Only just in time, sir.'

'I got held up.' Ken smiled as he opened the door and slid into the driving seat. 'They couldn't find the blessed suitcase. I'll have to put her in the car park, I suppose.'

'The short-term car park is down there on your left. You'll have to pay –'

The warden's sentence was drowned in the roar of the starting engine. Ken engaged Drive and moved fast away from the kerb. Out of the corner of his eye he saw the police constable turn and push his way into the Main Hall.

He drove down the hill, passed the entrance to the short-term car park and turned out towards the main London–

Brighton road. As he waited for a line of vehicles to pass, a police car, lights blazing, blue lamp flashing and siren screaming, came tearing down from the direction of Crawley and swung into the airport. He checked his watch. The time was 7.35 a.m. and opposite him was the first sign indicating the route back to London Airport.

He cut in mercilessly in front of a Hillman Hunter, whose driver flashed his lights angrily. Ken held the lever in second gear till the bonnet of the other car dwindled in his mirror. He was glad now that he had picked the fastest car in the Renta range. The 140 h.p. V8 engine could punch the robust vehicle from standstill to 60 m.p.h. in ten seconds and the maximum speed was in excess of 120 m.p.h. In case of emergency there were Girling disc brakes on all four wheels and for good measure the car was fitted with Dunlop Denovo failsafe tyres.

It was as he slowed for the roundabout at the end of the straight section of road that he realized he'd stepped into a car and driven off without experiencing an attack of the jitters. For the first time since he'd been trapped in his overturned, blazing Porsche 911 the terrible paralysis of fear, which immobilized him whenever he sat behind the wheel of a car, had vanished.

He began to concentrate on his driving. There would be time to work it all out in the aircraft. The vital thing now was to get back to Heathrow before the police net closed on the airport. Already the detective-sergeant must have put a call through from the chaplain's office. That was probably why the nearest patrol car had come screaming into Gatwick Airport. Five or ten minutes of search and enquiry would elicit the information that the suspect had left the area in front of the main entrance in a scarlet Rover V8 with black vinyl roof.

Had the warden got so far as to take down his number? Had the patrol car noticed the Rover as it turned in? How long would it take them to put out a general call? He could imagine the police network buzzing, 'Man aged about forty.

Height six foot. Slim build. Clean shaven, dark hair slightly curled at back. Wearing light-weight fawn suit. Driving scarlet Rover V8. Wanted for murder. Dangerous.'

He reckoned he had one advantage. Unless they could trace the car to Renta at London Airport they would not know that he was racing to Heathrow.

He had well and truly burned his boats now. Both the Italian and British police would be hunting him as a self-confessed murderer. Once again he was committed to an inescapable course of action by his own impulsive nature and an almost pathological incapacity to sit out a crisis.

He did not regret his decision to turn the table on Spurling and his inexperienced colleague. When he had seen what lay beneath the false bottom of that suitcase the truth had hit him. He knew he now had the explanation for the sequence of deaths which had started at Gatwick and continued through Venice, Padua, Verona, Milan and Como. As he let his speed rise to 100 m.p.h. on the narrow but straight road to Reigate the one thought uppermost in his mind was to make it back to that embattled castle above the Lake of Lugano. Nothing else in the world mattered.

And to think that during the long wait at Gatwick a week ago he had been on the point of abandoning the Italian Cities Tour and going home. He tried to recall the details of those four hours. Of course, now, endowed with hindsight, he could see the significance of incidents which had then seemed trivial.

CHAPTER II

'ALBION AIRWAYS regret to announce a further delay of one hour on their Flight 327 to Venice. Passengers on this flight may obtain refreshment vouchers from the Albion Airways desk.'

Ken Forsythe checked his watch as the girl's magnified voice echoed round the huge Main Hall at Gatwick Airport. After five already and the plane had been due to take off at three p.m.

'That's package tours for you,' the grey-haired man sitting beside him commented drily. 'These charter flights always have to take second place to the big airlines. Either that or some inspector's discovered that our plane's not airworthy.'

Ken had had time to study some of the people who would be his travelling companions. The couple sitting beside him were evidently retired folk who had become hardened package tourists. Mr Grant had the sunburned face and scalp of the dedicated amateur gardener, and his wife the expectant expression of a whist player waiting to be dealt a new hand.

Ken was beginning to regret the impulse which had made him decide to sample one of the much publicized package tours. He had picked out Connoisseur Air/Coach Tours from the pile of brochures the travel agency had pressed on him, and finally selected 'Cities and Lakes of Italy', a one-week tour which took in many of the places he had always wanted to see. It had all looked so attractive in the brochure, and he could enjoy the pleasures of motoring without having to get behind the wheel of a car.

He stood up, and placed his small suitcase on the seat.

'May as well see what the refreshment voucher amounts to.'

'It won't be much,' Mr Grant said, with a sniff. 'And of course the bar's not open yet.'

'Will you be staying here for a few minutes?'

Mr Grant nodded. His wife smiled motherly reassurance. 'I'll keep an eye on your bag for you. Mum and me will wait till they announce meal vouchers.'

Ken nodded his thanks and strolled over towards the information desk. Half a dozen passengers had got there before him. He was about to tack himself on to the back of the small queue when a woman came up from the opposite direction. Instinctively he held back to let her take the place in front of him. She gave him a quick glance and a smile of thanks.

As the queue edged towards the girl in the scarlet Albion Airways uniform he had the feeling that the woman was conscious of his eyes studying her from behind. That quick glance had awakened a response in him. Her hair was golden with russet tints and cut fairly short. It had a tousled look till you realized that this effect was the result of skilful hairdressing. Her mouth was, by strict fashion-magazine standards, rather on the large side, her nose slightly flat. The eyes were wide-set and expressive, the kind of eyes whose glance you could not meet casually.

She was elegantly but not flamboyantly dressed in a cream-coloured suit, with a wrap-over jacket secured by a tie-belt and a neat skirt that ended just above the knee. Her figure was very good indeed. He guessed that she was already into her thirties, but her skin was good, her body poised and lithe. He let his eyes run down her back. Slim waist, a well-defined but firm rump, beautifully shaped calves and ankles.

The other people in the queue were a good deal less encouraging. They included an intensely earnest and academic woman of perhaps forty whose incredibly thin, brown arms clutched a copy of *The Renaissance in Italy*, a belligerent-looking matron in a tweed suit and the harassed father of the two teenagers who had been annoying everyone by listening to pop music on their small, tinny transistor.

'May I see your ticket, please?' The Albion Airways girl made her request for the tenth time with the same patient and friendly smile. The woman in front of Ken snapped her blue suède handbag open, groped inside for a moment. She looked up at him.

'You'd better go on. I can't seem to find my ticket.'

A pleasant voice, with a subtle, low timbre. Without knowing why Ken became convinced that, like him, she was travelling alone.

He said: 'I'm in no hurry.'

'No. But the people behind you are.'

With a smile that was somehow a private communication to him she nodded at the queue. A self-righteous young man with protuberant ears and a prominent Adam's apple was making no secret of his impatience.

Ken showed his own ticket to the girl, received a small voucher and moved away. The woman in the tie-belt suit did not look up from her handbag and he did not turn round as he went back to the seat where he had left his bag.

'Mr Forsythe, isn't it?'

Ken stopped in his tracks. 'That's right,' he said to the girl in the turquoise-blue uniform of Connoisseur Tours.

'I'm Gabriella Laroma, your courier for this tour. I missed you when you checked in at the airport.'

'My loss,' Ken murmured with sincerity. Gabriella spoke English perfectly, although her olive skin and black lustrous hair made her Italian origin evident. She was small, dazzlingly attractive, and looked far too young to carry the responsibilities of a courier. The tambourine-shaped hat perched on the side of her head added to the impression of childish innocence and vulnerability. 'Will you be coming on the tour with us?'

'Yes, of course. You got your refreshment voucher all right, Mr Forsythe?' Conscious of the admiration in his expression she kept her tone businesslike, though friendly.

'I did. What exactly does it entitle one to?'

B

'A fruit drink or a cup of tea or coffee, whichever you prefer.'

'How very generous! I think I'll wait till the bar opens.'

'I don't blame you, but if there's much more delay we'll probably be issuing meal vouchers. All right? If there's any other problem just let me know.'

My problems are not such as you could solve, Ken thought. He said: 'Thanks. Can you tell me one thing? I thought the Lakes and Cities Tour was limited to twenty. Who are all these other people who'll be on the same plane?'

'There are several tours going out on this flight. Most of the passengers are on Adriatic or Central Italy tours. That's why we're trying to keep the Lakes and Cities together in this part of the hall. All right?'

Ken nodded and went back to reclaim the seat beside Mr Grant. Gabriella's eyes followed him for a moment. She was more interested in Ken than she had shown. He must be a good forty but she had come round after a series of wild and unhappy love-affairs to preferring the older man. This one looked as if he knew how to handle a woman, secure the best tables in restaurants, set up a love scene with champagne, soft lights and low music. She wondered what on earth he was doing on a package tour. Men like that usually travelled the Continent in executive jets or Ferrari coupés.

She ticked Ken's name on her list and was about to move on when a hand touched her arm.

'Excuse me, miss.'

She turned, trying to conceal the shiver which the contact had caused. She switched on her professional smile. This was the kind of passenger she had learned to humour.

'Yes, Mr Benson?'

'We've been told twice now that our flight has been delayed for an hour. What guarantee is there that at the end of the next hour the same announcement won't be made?'

He was one of those men whose age is hard to determine.

The smooth, pink cheeks looked as if they did not need shaving, or had been purged of hair by the application of tropical leaves after the fashion of South American Indians. The hair was wispy and slightly grey. Beady blue eyes peered out from behind gold-rimmed spectacles. His mouth was thin with lines of petulance at the corners and the lips were unconsciously twitching as if he was sucking the last of a lemon-flavoured lozenge. She put him down as an academic who spent most of his time in dusty libraries.

'We can't guarantee anything, Mr Benson. I can only assure you that the company regrets the delay and is doing all it can to find another aircraft.'

'I'm afraid that's not good enough,' he snapped back at her. 'Your brochure clearly promises trouble-free holidays and invites us to leave all our cares behind. I believe it would be perfectly feasible to bring an action against you under the Trades Description Act.'

Gabriella kept her temper. 'Humour them,' Mr Sampson was for ever insisting. 'Always humour them. And if there are complaints you can't handle, refer them to me.'

'I'm sorry you feel like that, sir,' she said, and despite herself a note of coldness crept into her voice. 'In the circumstances I think you ought to make your complaint to Mr Sampson, our Tours Manager.'

'Nothing he can say will alter the fact that a great many people are being subjected to the most disgraceful inconvenience.'

He blinked rapidly several times as if to quench tears and then twisted away.

You get them like that, Gabriella reflected, people whose nerves went completely to pieces if they were kept waiting beyond a certain point. That was why it was so important for her to get round and have a word with each member of her party, keep them happy, never let them guess how close to breakdown the whole system was.

The Prestons were just getting up to troop off and trade their vouchers for hot drinks. They were a family of four with a boy and a girl aged fourteen and fifteen respectively. She had already decided that they were hopelessly spoilt by a weak-willed mother, but with their florally-decorated blue jeans they did at least give a spicing of youthfulness to the party.

'You'll find the cafeteria on the first floor,' she advised them. She caught Mrs Preston's warning eye and refrained from directing her standard smile at Mr Preston. It was always a bit like walking the tight-rope, this business of being charming and friendly without giving the men the impression that you were ready to strip down and go to bed with them.

She checked the names on her list and nerved herself to approach the two elderly ladies sitting alone together. Mrs Hayward and Mrs Sloman had supplied themselves with a book and a magazine each for the journey. They were evidently seasoned travellers and accustomed to working in tandem. Their heads were always close together as they exchanged outrageously frank opinions of their travelling companions.

'Oh, *that's* all right, my dear.' Mrs Hayward responded to her reassurances in an astonishingly deep voice like a man's. 'We're having quite fun, watching everyone else work themselves up into a twitter. You'll get us there in the end, we know that.'

Mrs Rayburn, who looked like being the odd one out on this tour, seemed to have no one to talk to and the seat beside her was empty. Gabriella sat down on it.

'You haven't been to collect your voucher, Mrs Rayburn?'

The faded and pathetic old lady shook her head gently, as if fearful of dislodging the out-dated straw hat pinned to her greying hair.

'This bag's so heavy and I could never stand in the queue with it and I don't like to leave it unattended.'

Gabriella glanced down at the bucket-shaped bag into which Mrs Rayburn had stuffed all the things she thought she might need on the flight.

'Would you like me to look after it while you go and get your voucher?'

'No, thanks, dear.' Mrs Rayburn shook her head unhappily. 'I don't really fancy any refreshment, not till we get going anyway.'

'You're feeling all right, Mrs Rayburn?' Gabriella asked, a little disturbed by the woman's pallid complexion and nervously fluttering hands.

'Yes, dear, quite all right. You needn't worry about me. I have some pills in case I get a bad turn.'

Gabriella resisted the temptation to pat her hand reassuringly. Mrs Rayburn was the kind that longs for companionship yet somehow seems incapable of breaking the barrier that separates them from other people.

She continued her little goodwill tour unhurriedly, knowing that she had plenty of time to kill. There was no chance of the plane being ready for take-off till well after eight, but to tell the passengers this would have disastrous results. Far better to break it to them gently, hour by hour.

By standing near the stairway which led up to the upper floor where the dining-rooms, bar and cafeteria were situated she was able to intercept several of her party and have a few words with them.

Mrs Meredith, the woman with the expensive clothes and enviably chic hair-style, was smiling at some inner thought and responded to Gabriella's enquiry absent-mindedly.

Miss Foxell, whose minimal shift-like dress revealed nut-brown, knobbly knees and elbows, had one finger marking her place in the book on the Italian Renaissance. Intensely shy, she looked round nervously when Gabriella spoke to her.

'I was so looking forward to dining in Venice,' she said in a low, hurried voice. 'I suppose we'll miss that now.'

'I'm afraid so. But there will be tomorrow night.'

Mr Alan Tasker, of the Adam's apple and prominent

ears, was festooned with photographic impedimenta which
was presumably of great value since he was never separated
from it.

'I know it's not your fault,' he told her. 'One never sees
the people who are really responsible for these muddles.
But I must tell you frankly that this is an extremely
unfortunate start to what was supposed to be a holiday.'

Still smiling, Gabriella agreed with him. Anything to get
rid of him quickly. He would never get to the point of
putting his hand on a girl's breast or patting her bottom.
Too pious and self-righteous. But he could not control his
eyes, which slid over her body, trying to make her clothes
transparent. It was the kind of impersonal, yet lascivious
inspection which she could not stand. Better any day to be
seized with frank lustfulness and bundled into a haystack
or the recesses of a deep sofa.

She had ticked off fourteen of the twenty names on her
list. The others must have decided to save their vouchers
or perhaps they spurned them completely. She set off to
locate them.

Mr and Mrs Collins, she had observed already, liked to
keep themselves to themselves. They wore casual suits of
blue denim and remained welded to each other like Siamese
twins. Though the absence of a ring was no proof of anything, Gabriella was certain they weren't married. These
package tours provided a haven for many a couple who
wanted to spend a lot of time together, mostly in bed.
The young man must be in his early twenties. He had long,
rather attractive and curly fair hair and a luxurious, flow-
ing moustache. 'Mrs Collins', to Gabriella's feminine eye,
seemed to be the epitome of a sex-kitten.

'She should go on a diet,' Gabriella thought cattily. 'Take
a few pounds off her boobs and bum.'

But they were going to be no trouble, those two, and she
moved on to the two young ladies whose attitude to the
whole tour was one of breathless excitement. Doreen Wilkins
was the one with the freckles and turned-up nose. She was

a physiotherapist at a London hospital and her friend Alice Norman was secretary to the Registrar.

'The trouble is,' Alice said, 'I took my travel-sickness pills when I got to the airport and I'm afraid that with all this waiting the effect may wear off.'

'I don't think so. They usually last for quite a few hours and we should be in Venice by midnight.'

'Midnight!' Doreen exclaimed. 'As late as that?'

Gabriella realized she had given the game away and tried to cover up. 'Well, at the very latest. I hope it will be much earlier.'

That left only one couple, the Joneses. He was a small and stout but immensely strong man with the weather-beaten face of the outdoor worker. A farmer, perhaps, or a builder.

'Well, we were warned it might be like this, isn't it?' he told Gabriella in a resonant lilting voice which confirmed his Welsh origins. 'But the waiting doesn't worry us. There's plenty to look at.'

In fact, Mr Jones's eyes had at that moment fastened on a hostess of Caledonian Airways whose pleated mini-skirt was swaying attractively as she walked across the Main Hall.

'And what do we call you?' Mrs Jones demanded, but in a friendly tone. She was built like a front-row rugby forward, but her voice was musical and vibrant.

'I'm Gabriella Laroma. It's an Italian name but actually I was brought up in England –'

'Aye, that's not an English name,' Mrs Jones confirmed, nodding her silvery head. 'It would be too much of a mouthful for me. Is it all right if we just call you – what was that name again?'

'Gabriella. Please do. I'd much prefer it.'

'And I suppose you speak Italian as well as English?'

'Yes, I think I can say I do.'

'And you'll be showing us round all these sights and places we're going to?'

'That's right.'

Mr Jones had watched the tartan skirt out of sight and now let his gaze rest with pleasure on Gabriella's face.

'It must be interesting work, travelling about like that. How do you come to get a job like that, a slip of a girl like yourself?'

'Well,' Gabriella wondered how to express this without sounding too vain. 'I took a degree in Fine Arts. My special period was the Renaissance in Italy.'

'A degree at University?' Mrs Jones repeated in wonder, looking at Gabriella with awe and astonishment.

They were compulsive talkers. It was a good twenty minutes before she could break away from them and by that time the hour was nearly up. She felt that she could do with a little refreshment herself and went across to the Albion Airways desk.

'Any news about an aircraft?'

'They've got hold of a VC-10 from Caledonian,' the girl in the scarlet uniform told her, 'but it's having to fly down from Prestwick. You won't be taking off much before seven.'

'Four hours late,' Gabriella said. 'It has been worse.'

'Mr Sampson says we're going to give them a meal to keep them happy. I'll be making the announcement any minute now.'

'Give me a few minutes to grab a bite before you do. There will be a general stampede when they get their meal vouchers. And, by the way, if Sammie's in his office I'd like him to have a word with one of my passengers who's threatening the company with legal action.'

'Yes. He's there. You can go straight on in. He's got nobody with him at the moment.'

Mr Sampson, a plausible and quick-witted young man with dark, luxuriant hair, the latest in neckties and a suit of the most dashing cut, listened with amusement to her account of Mr Benson.

'Bring him along to me,' he said with cheerful confidence. 'I'll give him a bit of the old soft soap, offer him a free ticket on one of our day tours or something like that.'

When Gabriella went out into the Main Hall she wondered what alerted her senses to the change in the atmosphere of the place. The scene was one that had become very familiar to her. Passengers were spilling in through the arrival channels with that vaguely stupefied expression which air travel induces. Bewildered tourists, despairing of finding a porter to guide them, were promenading wire-framed trolleys, loaded with luggage and those plastics bags in which duty-free goods bought on the aircraft are wrapped. A queue of French students postured and gesticulated, chirruping like a cageful of birds, as they waited to pass through one of the departure channels. From behind the counters of the desks which surrounded the hall – airline companies, car hire firms, banks, magazine stands, tobacco stalls – faces looked out with politely impersonal expressions. An occasional porter in blue uniform, trundling a trolley, cut through the mass of drifting people with a whistle or a shout of warning.

'May I have your attention, please?' It was the voice of the girl at the Albion desk, the amplification of the speaker system allowing her to talk in a breathily confidential tone. 'Albion Airways regret to announce a further delay of an hour on their Flight 327 to Venice. Passengers on this flight may obtain a meal voucher on application to the Albion Airways desk. Thank you.'

Gabriella stole a look towards a seating area in the form of a three-sided square where a dozen of her group had settled themselves. She would have been willing to go over and face their complaints if at that moment the reason for the change of atmosphere had not become clear to her. A number of quiet men in dark suits had made their appearance in the Main Hall. There were perhaps only half a dozen of them but their manner was so purposeful that to the experienced eye they stood out like whippets in a flock of sheep.

Gabriella went across to the main information desk, noting on her way that the queue of French students was being passed at accelerated speed into the departure lounge and that the stream of people arriving from the railway station or car park had been sealed off.

'I see we've got the Force here,' she said to the clerk on duty. 'Not another drugs raid?'

'Something about a bomb. The police think it's a hoax, but they're checking to be on the safe side. I read in the paper that the IRA were threatening to carry their campaign to England, but they'd go for military targets – not an international airport.'

'Are they going to clear the place?' Gabriella asked anxiously. If the police evacuated the airport she would be lucky to get her party to Venice that night.

'It's not justified. We've had three of these in the past week. It's either some practical joker or a professional house-breaker who wants to know that the police are busy over here. You can't clear the airport every time.'

'I hope you're right.'

Gabriella turned away. This meant goodbye to the bite of food she had hoped for. She hurried towards the area where she had seen a group of her passengers sitting. One of the detectives was already talking to Mr Jones in a courteous but urgent voice. Gabriella saw that Mrs Jones and four or five others had left their places, presumably to go and collect their meal vouchers.

'Can I be of any help?' Gabriella said, cutting in on the conversation.

The detective turned round and immediately realized what her official position was.

'Yes, you can, miss. This is just a routine check. How many of these passengers can you identify?'

'All the ones in this area.' Gabriella's gesture included the open square lined with black, padded seats.

'They are all passengers whom you know to have booked in advance?'

'Yes.'

'Thank you.' The detective ran his eyes round the group. 'And can you all identify these pieces of luggage as your own?'

'Well,' Mrs Sloman said in her distinctly genteel voice, 'not exactly. You see, some people have gone to collect these vouchers the announcement was about. But this is Mrs Hayward's bag, I can vouch for that.'

'And this one belongs to my friend, Miss Norman,' Doreen Wilkins put in.

'The wife and I share this holdall,' Mr Jones said, patting a mock-leather, zip-up grip.

'And this is all our family stuff,' Mrs Preston said, pointing rather shamefacedly to the assortment of bags and clothing which littered the space occupied by her family. 'My husband and son have gone to collect the vouchers.'

The detective turned to Benson, who had just come back from the toilets and was sitting beside Mrs Rayburn. He looked rather alarmed at the whole thing.

'And you, sir?'

'I'm on my own, Officer.' Benson smiled nervously. 'And I believe in travelling light.'

'That seems to account for everything then,' the detective said. 'I needn't trouble you ladies and gentlemen any further.'

The officer moved on and instantly Gabriella was bombarded with questions.

'Oh, it's just a check they carry out from time to time, to verify who's in the airport, you know. In case of pick-pockets and that sort of thing.'

'Or drug-traffickers,' remarked Mr Jones in his strong, carrying voice.

Gabriella nodded wisely as if she knew he had hit the nail on the head and addressed herself to Mr Benson.

'I've arranged for Mr Sampson to hear your complaint, Mr Benson. If you'd like to come with me now —'

'Oh, I don't think there's much point in my —'

'Mr Sampson's waiting for you in his office,' Gabriella said very firmly. She had no intention of letting him off the hook now.

Benson glanced unhappily round the ring of faces, obviously reluctant to go through with his complaint.

'What are you afraid of?' Mrs Sloman had not only the features but the voice of a female archbishop. 'The young lady is giving you your chance. You can speak up for all of us while you're there, can't you?'

Reluctantly Benson got to his feet and followed Gabriella towards the office.

'Never pays to complain on these tours,' Mrs Sloman remarked to no one in particular. 'It only gets you into deeper water.'

'I liked the way she handled him,' Mr Jones said with relish, the leather seat squeaking as he twisted his broad behind. 'For all her charm she can crack the whip when she wants to, isn't it?'

Those who had been to collect the vouchers were trickling back, clutching the flimsy bits of paper in their hands.

'What about all our bags?' Doreen Wilkins said. 'Is it safe to just leave them here – especially if there are pickpockets about?'

'I'll stay here.' It was Mrs Rayburn who piped up in her quavering voice. 'In any case I could never eat a dinner at six o'clock.'

'But you may not get a meal on the aircraft,' Diana Meredith pointed out.

'I know, dear.' The old lady patted Diana's hand as if she was the one who needed reassurance. 'But all the same I'd rather not eat now. It would only upset me. I have to be so careful nowadays. The only thing is I don't know what to do with this key.'

'What key's that?'

'I found it in my bag and I know it's not mine.' She fumbled in the bucket-shaped bag and produced a small key with a number attached to it. 'I can't think how it got there. Do you think I ought to hand it in to the Lost Property?'

'I'll do that,' Diana said, putting out her hand to take the key. 'But I think I'll have dinner first. All the others have gone up already.'

'Thank you, my dear. Thank you ever so.'

From the top of the stairs she looked back at the old lady. The extraordinary straw hat with its brave bunch of cherries and faded red band was bent over her bag. She was hunting for her little bottle of pills. Diana could not explain to herself why she felt it was wrong to leave the old thing alone in the vastness of the Main Hall.

Ken Forsythe would have liked to find himself beside Diana Meredith at the dinner table. Instead he had to make do with the very smug Mr Tasker and the obviously academic Mr Benson. From the other side of the table the physiotherapist and her friend shot him quick glances over their soup and then began to talk in whispers.

The meal, of tasteless frozen food kept in reserve for such an occasion, was consumed at breakneck speed. As the other passengers trickled back to the seats they had marked with coats, magazines or luggage, Ken strolled into the dimly-lit bar. He thought a brandy might do something to help the cold chicken and ice-cream which he could feel working their way uneasily through his digestive system.

'Rémy Martin VSOP, sir?' the barman suggested, judging that he had a customer here who was selective about what he drank.

'That'll do fine. And I'll have one of those cigars, please.'

The barman served the brandy in a balloon-shaped glass and snapped his lighter for Ken's cigar. Ken swirled the liquid round, warming the glass with his cupped hand, and drew luxuriously on his cigar.

There was still time to pull out of this. Having seen something of the companions he would have for the next eight days, he was beginning to wonder if he had condemned

himself to a week of excruciating boredom. The woman he
had bumped into in the queue was the one bright spot.
Suppose it turned out that she was going on one of the
other tours? Still, he reminded himself sternly, he had not
come on this trip to pick up women. The object of the
exercise was to look at pictures, sculpture, architecture, to
see something of the cities which so far had only been names
in the history books of painting. He might as well go through
with it now.

'Your attention, please.' Even here in the dim intimacy
of the bar there was no escape from the relentless
young woman on the loudspeaker system. 'Albion Airways
announce the departure of their flight number 327 to
Venice. Will passengers please proceed to departure channel
number 2 immediately. All passengers on Flight 327 to
Venice to departure channel number 2 immediately, please.
Thank you.'

'Thank you for nothing,' Ken muttered. Just typical.
Keep you waiting for four hours and then start a panic at
the moment when you are settling down to enjoy a brandy
and cigar.

Deliberately taking his time and restraining the impulse
to hurry, he finished his brandy and put the glass back on
the counter. A third of the cigar was smoked and the first
half-inch of ash had dropped as he went at his own pace
down the stairs to the Main Hall.

There was no sign of his fellow passengers. They had
gathered up their belongings with obedient haste and gone
scuttling off to the departure lounge. Ken rescued his copy
of *Classic Car* from the seat where he had left it and strolled
towards the exit marked Departure Channel Number 2.

Gabriella was waiting at the exit and her expression made
it clear that she was exasperated by Ken's casual response
to the announcement.

'I thought we were going to have to leave you behind,
Mr Forsythe.'

'You wouldn't do that, surely. What's all the rush about, suddenly?'

'We've got clearance for take-off in twenty minutes. If we miss that we may have to wait another hour. Traffic's very heavy tonight. You haven't seen Mrs Rayburn, have you?'

'Mrs Rayburn? I wouldn't know if I had. So I'm not the last then?'

'You may be. If she doesn't come soon we're just going to have to leave without her. Will you go on through Gate Number 1?'

As he went through the emigration check-point Ken could hear the voice of the girl on the loudspeaker system suggesting in veiled terms that Mrs Rayburn had better stir her stumps and convey her sorry old limbs to the departure lounge forthwith.

There was no time to buy any liquor or smokes in the duty-free shop. His fellow passengers were already trooping down the quarter-mile corridor that would take them to the bay where the VC-10 awaited. With his long stride, Ken was easily able to overhaul half of them before the stairway that led on to the tarmac. As he climbed the mobile ladder to the doorway, he could see that Diana Meredith was a few places in front of him.

'Welcome aboard, sir,' the pert little hostess said as he reached the top. 'Mind your head.'

People were still standing about, taking off their over-coats, shoving packages and parcels under their seats. Ken pushed through them till he was half-way along the gang-way, saw that Diana Meredith had found a seat by the porthole and that the one next to her was empty. As he reached it Mr Tasker made a move to sit down.

'Excuse me,' Ken said firmly. 'I think that's my seat.'

While Tasker's jaw dropped, Ken slipped quickly past him, sat down and gave the man his most friendly smile. It was not returned and Ken knew that he had made one certain enemy for the duration of the tour.

He turned to Diana Meredith. 'You weren't keeping this seat for anyone, were you?'

She shook her head, unable to prevent herself from smiling at his presumptuous assurance. Her eyes dropped to the magazine on his lap. If she had been expecting to see a copy of *Playboy*, *Men Only* or *Mayfair*, she was disappointed. The very masculine full-frontal view of a supercharged Bentley 4½ litre glared at her from the cover.

'May I have your attention, please?' This time the voice came through on the internal system of the VC-10, more muted and intimate than in the airport hall. 'Does anyone know anything about Mrs Rayburn? She's the lady who was wearing the blue coat and the straw hat with a bunch of cherries on it.'

A silence had fallen in the aircraft, broken only by the giggles of the Preston kids, for whom the bunch of cherries was a huge joke.

'She promised to stay and look after our luggage while we had dinner,' the strong voice of Mrs Hayward replied from somewhere at the back. 'But when we came back she had gone, raffia bag and all. Fortunately nothing had been stolen. Nothing of ours anyway.'

The captain had come through the door from the flight deck. He waited till Mrs Hayward's voice had trailed away.

'Any relatives or friends of hers on board?'

There was no reply. People looked round as if they thought they might spot by intuition a relation or friend of Mrs Rayburn. The captain shrugged his shoulders and gave a short nod.

A moment later the door of the aircraft thudded and the note of the engines rose as the pilot began to taxi out to the end of the runway.

At 7.35, just four hours and thirty-five minutes after its scheduled time, Albion Airways Flight 327 for Venice became airborne.

CHAPTER III

THE OFFICE of the airport chaplains at Gatwick is situated beneath the Main Hall, down the moving staircases which lead to the toilets and the exit to the coach station.

It was just after eight when the Reverend Christopher Hinkley, the C of E chaplain, descended the moving staircase. It always irked him that the office of the chaplains should be relegated to the area considered fit for lavatories, telephone booths and lockable left-luggage compartments, whilst overhead the banks, magazine stands and tobacco kiosks pandered to the less commendable aspects of human nature. He had just returned from dealing with one of those unpredictable problems which are inevitably referred to the chaplain. Not strictly speaking Church work at all, but an airport is an area of stress and human crisis, and if the chaplain declined to deal with these problems, who would?

This time it had been an Italian girl still in her teens, who had seen her lover off on his plane and then gone back to the Ladies on the upper floor, near the cafeteria, and tried to cut her wrists with a steak knife stolen from the cutlery stand. Hinkley had done what he could to calm the sobbing and hysterical girl till the arrival of the doctor, who gave her a sedative injection and expertly bandaged her bleeding wrists. He was relieved when the doctor decided that this was a case for hospitalization. That gave him a chance at last of snatching a much delayed evening meal.

He put his key in the lock of his door, tried to turn it and found that it was unlocked. He frowned in annoyance. Father Blake, who was standing in for his regular Roman Catholic colleague, had this tiresome habit of forgetting to lock the door. An admirable priest but head too high in the clouds to bother about such trivialities as locks, keeping the office tidy, putting the telephone back properly on its cradle.

C

He pushed the door open and entered the small office. Just room for a table, some chairs, a filing cabinet and the metal locker where the priests kept the surplices they wore for Sunday services. He stared suspiciously at the object which lay on the floor near the radiator. It was a battered straw hat, decorated by a bunch of cherries and a faded red band.

Now, who could have left that here? Perhaps some member of Father Blake's migrant flock or even someone who had found the door unlocked and crept in for a moment of peace and quiet.

He picked it up and hesitated. His conscience told him that he ought to take it and hand it straight in to the Lost Property Office. But it was already past the time for his evening meal. The hat could wait till tomorrow.

He put a hand out to open the locker and frowned again. It was locked and furthermore Father Blake had removed the key. There was no sign of it on the desk or window sill. Now, why should a man leave the door of the room open but lock the surplice cupboard? Perhaps he had stored something there which he did not want his Anglican colleague to see.

Oh well, he would just have to hope that Father Blake would replace the key before the following Sunday. He opened an empty drawer of the filing cabinet, popped the hat inside and promptly forgot all about it.

'This is your captain speaking, ladies and gentlemen. We have now reached our ceiling and are flying at an altitude of 32,000 feet. Our speed is 530 miles per hour and our course is approximately east-south-east. The weather is clear and we have every prospect of good visibility over the Alps. The lights you can see below on the port side are Paris.'

Diana Meredith lowered her book and glanced enquiringly at the man sitting beside her.

'Do you want to see Paris?'

'I'd rather see it from closer to,' he said, smiling and

closing his magazine. They were the first words exchanged between them since the aircraft had taken off from Gatwick, two hundred miles behind them. The air hostesses had been busily moving up and down the gangway, supplying the needs of the passengers, and now the lights had been turned down so that those who wanted to do so could sleep. The youthful Mr Collins had tilted his seat back almost into Ken's lap and his nubile companion had spread herself across his chest with one arm round his neck. Mr Grant had made his way to the toilet and back, the Preston kids, after a couple of raids up and down the gangway, had curled up like puppies and gone to sleep.

Ken had made up his mind that he was not going to rush this. His neighbour was not the kind of woman who would want to give the impression that she was easy. There was a reserve and wariness about her which made him realize that he could spoil everything by a clumsy remark. He knew that he had behaved outrageously in grabbing the seat beside her and must allow time for the initial impression to wear off. In his mind he had decided that he would make no move till they were descending to land at Venice Airport.

But now that she had given him an opening it would be impolite not to take it.

'You know Paris?' he said.

'Only as a visitor. My husband used to go there quite often on business trips. Sometimes I went along too and took the chance of visiting museums and art galleries.'

She had mentioned her husband very early in the conversation. Was that intended as a warning to keep his distance?

'You're interested in pictures and that sort of thing? That's what made you come on this tour?'

'Yes. I've no expert knowledge but I love just looking at beautiful things. It doesn't have to be pictures, it can be buildings, sculpture, embroidery, even furniture. I've never been to Italy and this chance to visit several centres of art quite cheaply was too good to miss.'

'And your husband doesn't mind sparing you for a week?'

Ken laid the question on the line as lightly and as casually as he could. After all, it was she who had brought him into the conversation.

'I haven't a husband – not any more.'

She said it in an impersonal way, as if she were speaking of a car or an old fur coat.

'Oh, I'm sorry –' he began awkwardly, cursing himself for putting his foot in it.

'It's all right,' she said, quickly and brightly. 'You needn't offer me condolences or anything. We're divorced now.'

'You sound,' Ken said carefully, deciding to take the risk and move further on to this personal and intimate territory, 'as if it hadn't happened long ago.'

'It seems a long time.' She was looking away from him now, back at the lights of Paris which were slowly receding past the port wing. 'In fact, it's only ten months.'

'Ten months can be a hell of a long time. It's something other people don't seem to understand. That for them time is passing at its normal speed and for you every day is like a month.'

Her head had turned again and she was looking at his profile. Between forty and forty-five, she was thinking. Certainly five, maybe ten years older than Henry, and with a lot more strength and character in his face. But she could see by his eyes, and the lines around them, that he had endured some very painful experience.

'Don't tell me you're divorced too.'

'No. My wife died. It's quite a while ago now. She was only thirty. At the time I thought –'

He stopped. Suddenly he knew that his voice was going to go funny, even after three years. What an extraordinary thing, that he had nearly blurted out to a completely strange woman what he had never confided to anyone.

She had begun a quick gesture, as if to put a hand on his arm, and checked herself just in time.

'I'm sorry. I'm afraid that was very clumsy of me. Thinking so much of my own misfortunes that I forgot other people have had to face much worse ones.'

'It's all right.' Ken had recovered himself immediately. 'Several years have passed since it happened.'

But it's been a long haul back, she thought.

'Do you have any children?'

Ken shook his head. 'No. No children. Just as well really, I suppose.'

'Maybe. I often think that if Henry and I had had children we might have made more of a go of it. But I'm not convinced. And if our marriage had still failed the children would have been the ones to suffer. So perhaps it was for the best.'

Silence fell. It was as if they were both startled that at the very outset of the conversation they had touched on the most intimate aspects of their lives.

Ken saw the hostess start to move down the aisle, ready to deal with sickness, thirst or just plain flirtation.

'What do you say to a drink?' he suggested.

'I think that's a good idea,' she replied with a smile.

'What would you like?'

'Well, I've always been convinced that there's only one thing to drink in the air and that's champagne. But half a bottle will be enough for two.'

Ken nodded in satisfaction. No beating about the bush. He liked a woman who came straight out with what she wanted. He put out a hand to stop the hostess.

'Do you have any champagne?'

'Yes,' the girl answered hesitantly. 'I think we have.'

'In half bottles?'

'Well, I'm not sure about half bottles . . . We have it in quarters.'

'Bring whatever you have. If you haven't any half bottles we'll have two quarters.'

'And two glasses?' the girl asked, glancing tentatively at Diana, as if she half expected a cry for rescue from that direction.

'Yes, two glasses,' Ken said firmly.

'Doesn't it strike you as strange,' Diana said, ten minutes later, as he filled her glass for the second time, 'that until a quarter of an hour ago we had not exchanged a word and already we've confided the most intimate details to each other – and drinking champagne on top of it.'

'Doesn't strike me as strange at all,' Ken said. 'We've both lived enough to know about people. When you realize that you're absolutely on a wave-length with someone why waste time on trivialities?'

'You speak as if this was a frequent experience for you,' Diana said. There was a sudden hint of coldness in her voice, which warned him that she was still very much a stranger, despite the sudden flow of magnetic current which he had felt passing between them.

'I assure you,' he said with emphasis, 'that it is not a frequent experience for me. Rather, I would say, a unique experience.'

The captain's voice on the loudspeakers conveniently punctuated a remark which Ken felt might have sounded too intense.

'We will be crossing the Alps in a few moments, ladies and gentlemen. We may encounter a little air turbulence, but it's nothing to worry about. You may feel more secure if you fasten your seat-belts and I'd advise you to keep an eye on any cups or glasses. Weather reports from Venice are good and we should be landing in about forty minutes.'

The Fiat coach which would provide the conveyance for the Cities and Lakes tour had been waiting at the airport for five hours when the VC-10 finally landed at around midnight. Connoisseur Tours had ascertained by means of a consumer research study that it gave their clients a sense of security to have an English-speaking driver on these foreign travels. In fact Joe, who had been brought up in Clapham, had married an Italian girl from Trieste. He spoke a fluent though highly indivualistic brand of Italian.

Even after the long wait he was still in a good mood. He had filled in some of the time by chatting up one of the waitresses in the airport cafeteria and was pretty sure that he had now filled the vacancy created in Venice by his row with Concetta. To Joe it was a matter of honour to have a woman in each of the six cities figuring on the Connoisseur Tour. This did not in the least affect his devotion to the mother of his four children.

He greeted Gabriella with his usual cheeky wink and saw the travel-weary passengers aboard his coach with the air of a destroyer captain receiving a delegation of VIPs in some foreign port.

While Captain Berlin and his crew took their aircraft back to Prestwick, Gabriella had resumed responsibility for her party, now weaned from the larger groups destined for the Adriatic and Central Italy.

As Joe eased the coach out of the embussing area she unhooked the microphone from the dashboard. Standing at the front of the bus and supporting herself with a hand on the back of the single seat reserved for the courier she launched into her customary briefing.

'If I could have your attention for a few minutes, ladies and gentlemen.'

A respectful silence fell and all faces were turned up towards her. She saw that Mr Forsythe and Mrs Meredith had separated and were sitting on different sides of the gangway. The Preston kids were looking dog-tired and Mrs Sloman's complexion had turned a very worrying shade of greeny-yellow. Paradoxically, the brightest of the whole party was Mr Benson, whose spectacles gleamed at her from the third seat back.

'As you know, we very much regret the delay, but I have been in touch with the hotel and I am told that a cold

meal and refreshments will be waiting for you in your
rooms. We will adjust tomorrow's programme to give you
plenty of time to have a good night's sleep.'

She glanced down at Joe and saw his mouth twitch into
a smile.

'Of course, I don't have to tell you that there are no
motor vehicles in Venice, so the coach will take you across
the lagoon to Piazzale Roma and from there you will be
conveyed to the hotel by *motoscafo*. The whole journey
should not take much more than an hour.'

Ken glanced at his watch. They should be there by
one a.m. Not so bad, all things considered. He tilted his seat
back and stretched his legs. The bus had space enough to
allow a few single seats to those who were not travelling
with companions. After leaving the aircraft he had made
no attempt to stick close to Diana Meredith. He did not
want to make her feel he was crowding her. She was sitting
a little way back on the other side.

The arrival in Venice by moonlight was magical and
compensated for the long delay at Gatwick. As the coach
purred along the causeway which linked the island city to
the mainland the calm waters of the lagoon stretched like
quicksilver on either side. Ahead the towers and roofs of the
city rose gradually against the sky.

The trip by motor launch through the canals offered a
rare opportunity to see Venice in its quietest of moods.
Even the Gran Canale was almost deserted, and only an
occasional light shone from the windows of the *palazzi* lining
the waterway. Now and again they passed a façade floodlit
with golden or mauve light, sometimes the shouts and
laughter of some party burst out from an open window and
there were still occasional gondolas flitting mysteriously
through the shadows, bearing lovers or gourmets who had
supped and wined on the water.

The Hotel Ruffino was in a quiet canal not far from the
Piazza San Marco, and when Ken opened the windows of
his bedroom he found that he was looking straight across

at a magnificent Byzantine palace.

It was so magical that, when he had consumed what he wanted of the cold meal provided, he rang room service, ordered a bottle of chilled Frascati wine and sat drinking it on the balcony till two a.m.

'Is this all they give us for breakfast?' Mrs Jones was contemplating the carefully planned ration which had been placed before her – two rolls and some sticks of bread in crisp paper, a couple of squares of butter in neat wrapping, the tiny parcels of sugar and the round plastic containers of every sort of jam except marmalade. She had unwisely put on a pair of scarlet trousers and her rear view looked more than ever like that of a rugger forward.

'This is what's called a continental breakfast,' Mr Grant explained gently.

The Grants and Joneses were seated at one of the tables in the section of the dining-room which the management had reserved for the Connoisseur Tour. They had been first down and had bagged the best table, looking out over the canal.

Gabriella was hovering about, ready to help, as her party trickled in ones and twos across the foyer from the lift doors and into the sunny dining-room. This first meal of the tour always needed watching. The hotels inevitably wanted her people sitting at tables of four or six and if awkward groupings were formed now it could spread an uneasy atmosphere through the whole tour.

The Grants and Joneses were getting on all right together, so she needn't worry about them. Miss Foxell, Mr Benson and Mr Tasker came in separately and let themselves be directed by the waiter to the same table. That left one extra seat. When Mrs Meredith came in Gabriella would have liked to signal to the waiter to put her at an empty table and start a new group, but the man obstinately insisted on placing her beside Mr Tasker, on whom she bestowed a friendly smile.

The Prestons came in all together, having got up at dawn and gone on a walking tour of the quarter. Mrs Hayward and Mrs Sloman, clad now in sack-like cotton dresses suitable for hot climates, sailed in with their faint air of intellectual superiority and insisted on being placed beside the window. When the two Collinses came in everybody turned to have a covert look at them. They were wearing their identical blue denim suits and looked as if they had spent the night wide awake on cloud nine. With that strange instinct of package tourists their fellow-passengers had picked up the torrid sexuality which the couple exuded and had not been kidded for one moment by the title of 'Mrs'.

The asinine waiter plonked them down beside Mrs Hayward and Mrs Sloman, who nodded coldly and edged their chairs a little farther away. Gabriella decided that she would have to do something to break that group up.

When the two young women, Miss Norman and Miss Wilkins, came in she knew that her party was complete, with one exception. Mr Forsythe had not appeared. She was wondering whether she ought to get the telephone operator to ring through to his room when she saw his head pass the window and a minute later he came in.

'Not too late again, I hope?' he said. 'It was such a beautiful morning that I thought I'd go for a walk before breakfast.'

'You're last again, I'm afraid,' she told him with a laugh, noticing that his eyes explored the room till they found Diana Meredith. 'But we're not starting the tour till ten, so you've plenty of time. There's a seat at that table with Miss Norman and Miss Wilkins.'

The two girls gave Ken embarrassed glances and Doreen Wilkins blushed faintly as Ken took one of the two empty chairs at their table. He caught Diana's eye across the room and they exchanged a brief smile.

That left one empty chair, which should have been occupied by Mrs Rayburn. Mrs Sloman's eye rested on it

and she made an imperious signal, summoning Gabriella
to her side.

'Will Mrs Rayburn be following on later?' she demanded,
and then, not waiting for an answer, ploughed on. 'We
think it was disgraceful the way that poor woman got left
behind. Four hours' delay and then you had us scrambling
into the aircraft like refugees from a war zone.'

'If we can arrange for her to rejoin the tour we will,
Mrs Sloman. It was a rush, I know, but circumstances were
beyond our control. We decided we really had to give you
a meal but no sooner were you all in the dining-room than
the Control Room gave us a departure time. Now, I'm
sorry, but you'll have to excuse me, please.'

She had seen the manager at the door of the dining-room
and by the look on his face he was in a hurry to speak to
her.

It turned out to be a call from Mr Sampson at Gatwick.
She took it in the manager's office.

'Christ, I've had a job to get through to you! It would
have been almost quicker to fly out and give you the
message personally.'

'Sorry.' Gabriella had developed the habit of accepting
blame to such an extent that now she was even doing it with
Sammie. 'I've been here all the time.'

'Oh, it's not *your* fault. Listen, you know that Rayburn
woman you had to leave behind?'

'Yes. I've been worrying about her. Some of my
passengers are quite incensed about it. They think we should
have waited for her –'

'You'd have had to wait a long time.'

'You mean she changed her mind?'

'Must have done. She didn't answer any of the calls,
even after your flight had taken off. She's completely
vanished.'

'I thought she seemed worried about herself. Wouldn't
have any dinner in case it upset her. And I don't suppose

the long wait helped. Perhaps she just decided to give the tour a miss. Have you tried her home address?'

'I phoned the number she gave and there was no reply. I'll try again later. It's a bit worrying.'

'Do you think I ought to tell the other passengers?'

'Is there any point? Why not just let them forget her?'

'They haven't forgotten her. Some of them want to know what we're going to do about leaving her behind.'

'Then you'd better tell them she changed her mind. Something like that. Play it down as much as you can.'

'You can bet your life I'll do that,' Gabriella said with feeling.

'If I could have your attention for a moment –' Gabriella had to make the plea a couple of times before Mr Jones came to her rescue with a loud command to 'give the young lady a chance to speak, everybody'.

The nineteen members of the group had assembled in the foyer of the Hotel Ruffino. They had apparelled themselves in the incongruous and sometimes ridiculous garments which the British consider *de rigueur* in any country with a reputation for a hot climate.

Venice this morning had come up to expectations and the brilliant sunshine was already pushing waves of heat through the doorway of the air-conditioned hotel. The knowing ones, like Miss Foxell and Mrs Grant, had brought little shawls or cardigans to put over their bare shoulders when they entered the cold interiors of churches. Mr Tasker, still in collar and tie and tweed jacket, was laden with the equipment of the complete amateur photographer, two cameras, a box of lenses and other mysterious appliances in leather cases.

'Well, ladies and gentlemen,' Gabriella began when the hum of conversation died down. 'This is really the start of our tour so let me say welcome to Venice, or if you have been here before, welcome back again. As you know, we shall be spending two days here before going on to Padua.

Then, after Verona, we have a tour round the Lake of
Garda before going on to Milan. After Milan we pay a
visit to Como and its lake, and on the way to Turin we shall
see something of the Lake of Lugano and the Lakes of
Varese, Orta and finally Lago Maggiore.'

Gabriella paused and smiled out at the sunshine as if it
were an intimate ally.

'Venice, you know, has been called the Queen of the Sea.
That is because she rose from the sea and her power
depended on the sea. The first Venetians were fishermen
who laid wattles and built huts for themselves on the mud
banks of the lagoon. Later, when the hordes of Attila
plundered the mainland, these small artificial islands provided refuge and safety. So that by 1200 a great city had
grown here and in succeeding centuries her power extended
to Constantinople and throughout the whole Mediterranean.
And with power came wealth and with wealth a munificent
patronage of the arts. That was why every year the Doge
used to go forth on to the waters of the lagoon in his
splendid barge, the *Bucintoro*, and cast a ring into the waves
to symbolize the marriage of Venice with the sea. And, it
was because of the wealth of its merchants that artists,
sculptors and architects flourished here and were able to
produce so many masterpieces that Venice can claim to
be the first art gallery in the world.'

Full marks to Connoisseur Tours, Ken thought, for
securing a courier who could also talk so eloquently about
the places visited. Now that she was back on her native soil
Gabriella seemed to have bloomed and softened. The way
she walked had become more sensuous, her curves seemed
to have filled out ever so slightly and the faint Italian
flavour, more in the intonation than in the pronunciation,
had become more evident in her speech. Ken found that it
gave her little lectures a special charm and was particularly
appropriate when the subject of her talk was Italian art.
He hoped that they were paying her a whacking salary,
because she was really doing two jobs in one. He could

see that Mr Jones in front of him had been completely captivated by the dark, eager face and the confiding lilt of the Mediterranean voice. The Welshman was wearing an almost transparent nylon shirt through which could be seen his string vest.

'So first,' Gabriella concluded her introduction, 'we will go to Piazza San Marco, where you will see the Basilica and the Palace of the Doges.'

'You said there were no cars or buses in Venice,' Mr Grant said cleverly, like the dull boy in the class who thinks he can catch teacher out. 'I've been looking at the map and we're quite a way from the centre here. How are we supposed to get there?'

'We have a *motoscafo* to the Molo,' Gabriella reassured him sweetly, 'and from there we walk, as the Venetians themselves do. Most places in the city are near enough to be within walking distance. And since Venetians do not hurry they are able to cultivate walking as an art. Now, if you are all ready –'

By mid-morning Ken was bemused. The constant presence of water, shimmering and stirring in the dazzling light, the murmur of hundreds of voices in the Piazza San Marco, the hordes of pigeons strutting fearlessly among people's legs, the fleshy tints of the Palazzo Dogale, the sheer profusion of architectural and artistic richness had given him the same heady feeling as some magical vintage of wine, which could at the same time intoxicate and yet sharpen every sense.

As the conducted tour entered the Ducal Palace he deliberately hung back to let them get ahead. Fascinating as Signorina Gabriella's exposition was, he wanted for a while to take things at his own speed, stop and just stare vacantly if he felt like doing so.

To his annoyance he heard a step behind him and, turning, found that someone else had the same idea.

The gold-rimmed spectacles of Mr Benson glinted at him

from beneath a faded straw hat. Today he was wearing a fawn tropical suit, rather baggy round the legs and with pockets which had sagged from the weight of spectacle cases, smoking accoutrements and notebooks.

'That's the trouble with these tours,' Benson remarked in a friendly tone. 'They rush you through everything so. Tintoretto's *Paradiso* in the Sala del Maggior Consiglio is the largest oil painting in the world, and yet you're supposed to drink it all in during the time it takes you to walk past it.'

'You know Venice already then?'

Benson smiled deprecatingly. 'This is my fourth visit. But I can never have too much of it. I come on these package tours because they represent the best value for money. But there is no rule which says you must listen to every word the guide says.'

They had walked through the passage that led to the Cortile of the Palace. The tail-enders of the party were just disappearing up the Scala d'Oro towards the main floor.

'Though as guides go our Signorina is not at all bad.'

'Oh, very toothsome, I'll grant you that!' Benson agreed with surprising warmth. 'And knows her stuff too. She told me that she had studied Fine Arts at Sussex University and Padua. You know the Scrovegni Chapel, of course?'

'This is my first trip to Italy,' Ken confessed.

'Oh dear me!' Benson stopped to gaze at Ken in pained surprise. 'What a lot you have to make up for – and on a package tour too. Be guided by me, sir. Select one or two things and give them your full attention. Here, for instance, one must ignore these grotesque figures and gigantic statues, pass unseeingly through the rooms of the *piano nobile* and then enter the Sala del Maggior Consiglio with untarnished eyes.'

Ken was beginning to regret the impulse which had made him hang back. It looked as if he had exchanged one guide for another and despite Benson's obvious expertise he preferred Gabriella's unassuming charm.

Under a sun that was now really fierce they crossed the Courtyard and ascended the superb stairway in the corner. It was a relief to enter the comparatively cool and spacious rooms.

Benson had paused in a doorway and gripped Ken's arm. 'Now!' he exclaimed. 'Now, you can open your eyes. Look at the proportions of this room. What size! What magnificence! And there it is! Tintoretto's masterpiece!'

Ken walked slowly towards the huge composition on the east wall and kept going until the picture filled his whole field of view.

'Yes!' Benson approved enthusiastically. 'That is what one must do. Walk into it, become absorbed in its passion, its force, its warmth.'

Feeling at the same time embarrassed and inadequate, Ken stood there for several long minutes, exploring the fresco with his eyes, while Mr Benson applied a pocket inhaler to each nostril in turn.

'Paradise,' he murmured, almost to himself. 'It's curious, isn't it, that even the greatest artists can only depict paradise in terms of what is best in the world we know.'

'Ah yes! That is true! But nowhere in our real world will you find so harmonious an arrangement of forms and colours as you have here.'

'We're getting left behind by the others,' Ken pointed out uncomfortably. 'They were just leaving here as we came in.'

'Probably gawping at the Bridge of Sighs,' Benson said scornfully. 'Its interest is purely macabre. What sort of person is fascinated by those terrible dungeons where human beings were left to rot in the damp and often flooded cells of the Prigioni Nuove? If you want to join them, please do. I intend to linger a little longer with Tintoretto and Veronese.'

Ken caught up with the group just as they were leaving the Ducal Palace. One member at least had noticed his absence. Diana Meredith gave him a look of mock disapproval and shook an admonishing finger at him. She was

looking very cool in a shirt-jacket with red buttons and
piping and a pair of cotton denim trousers with matching
red stripes. He took the cue to go and walk beside her as
Gabriella led her party to the landing-stage from which
their launch would take them back to lunch at the Hotel
Ruffino.

'We saw you,' she told him. 'You'd better be careful or
Miss Gabriella won't allow you to attend her classes any
more.'

'Did she notice? Perhaps I ought to apologize to her.
Actually I was taken in charge by another guide back
there!'

'Oh? Equally attractive?'

'Hardly that. It was our own Mr Benson, you know, the
one who looks like a classical scholar.'

'Oh, him.' Diana wrinkled her nose. 'He tried to button-
hole me after breakfast. What with him and Mr Tasker
I'm not going to be left in peace much.'

'Men who don't know when they're not wanted,' Ken
said, with a taste of bitterness in his throat. 'I suppose I'm
on the list too.'

'You don't force yourself on people.' She turned to look
at him appraisingly. 'In fact, I was wondering if I'd said
something to offend you. You seem to have been avoiding
me ever since we got off that plane.'

She had a trick of raising one eyebrow slightly. He found
it very provocative and wondered whether it was entirely
unconscious.

'If I've given that impression I'll see what I can do to
put it right. Let's make sure of sitting together for lunch.'

Any chance of a private conversation over lunch was
wrecked when the waiter, whose judgement of character
must have been the worst in the entire catering trade, placed
Mrs Hayward and Mrs Sloman beside them. Ken watched
Miss Foxell come in and hesitate between the table where
Miss Wilkins and Miss Norman were sitting, or the other

where Mr Benson and Mr Tasker were already ensconced.

'It's a funny thing,' he said to Diana, leaning across the table, 'but I keep thinking of everyone by their surnames and titles. I suppose they *do* have Christian names.'

Mrs Hayward overheard the remark and exchanged a look with Mrs Sloman which said: 'Just let him try using Christian names with *me*.'

'I know,' Diana agreed, watching the couple in blue denim suits come in. 'But I can't bring myself to think of those two as Mr and Mrs Collins. To me they're Jim and Jean.'

'Are those their real names?'

'Yes. I got to know them a bit better during this morning's tour. And Mr Tasker has asked me to call him Alan.'

'I know it's Doreen Wilkins and Alice Norman and I can see myself calling them by their first names, but I think la Foxell will be permanently Miss to me.'

Ken saw Mrs Hayward give a faint start and realized that Mrs Sloman had kicked her under the table. Gabriella was going round making sure that everyone was happy and had stopped at the table behind, where the Grants and Joneses were sitting. Something about the conversation had alerted Mrs Sloman. Ken broke off to listen too.

'Mrs Grant didn't get a wink of sleep,' Mr Grant was saying. 'It went on all night and you couldn't close your ears to it. We might as well have been in the same room.'

'I'll see the management and have your room changed if that's possible,' Gabriella promised him.

'I hope it is,' Mrs Grant said quaveringly. 'I don't know if I could face another night in that room.'

'Don't worry, Mrs Grant. I'm sure we can arrange something.'

As Gabriella moved on Ken noticed that she was blushing a little and taking great care not to look in the direction of Jim and Jean. Mrs Sloman met Mrs Hayward's eye and simply nodded, as if some theory she had propounded earlier had just been confirmed.

'There's a coffee bar just round the corner,' Ken said as they were moving out of the dining-room. 'What about going and having an Espresso somewhere with a bit more Venetian atmosphere?'

'Have we got time? We're supposed to be going to the Accademia, aren't we?'

'We've got half an hour. Our signorina does not require us till half past two.'

They went through the foyer and out into the sunlight, which was now really hot.

'She's what I would call a really beautiful woman,' Diana said, putting a hand up to shield her eyes from the glare. 'But I never know what men think. Do you think she's attractive – sexually, I mean?'

'Gabriella? Very attractive,' Ken said with feeling. 'Disturbingly so.'

'Why disturbing?' Diana asked, turning to watch his face closely as he answered.

'I'm not sure,' Ken said slowly, realizing that he could not say outright that he had several times tried to work out exactly what Gabriella would look like stripped of her clothes. 'Perhaps it's the combination of such physical beauty combined with an impression of remoteness.'

'She might not be all that remote if it came to the point. Have you thought of trying?'

'I should think every man on this tour has,' Ken said with a laugh. 'Except perhaps Mr Benson. I can't imagine him having a sex life.'

'She's got that amazing glow of youth. It passes so quickly. You don't realize how little time there is and suddenly – it's gone.'

'It can be replaced by something equally fascinating,' Ken said quietly. 'Here's the coffee bar. I hope we can get a seat.'

It was one of those tiny little shallow bars opening directly on to the footway. Reflected light from the moving surface of the canal outside rippled like waves on the ceiling. They were lucky to find a small table just behind the door. '*Due espressi, per favore,*' Ken told the waiter.

'I thought you said you hadn't been to Italy before,' Diana observed.

'I haven't. I learned a smattering of Italian along with a couple of other languages. I thought it would help me with my business.'

'Oh?' she said with genuine interest. 'What is your business?'

'Was,' he corrected her bluntly. 'I don't have a business any more.'

She leant back and waited till the *cameriere* had placed a tiny measure of strong black coffee and a glass of iced water before her. She realized that she had broken an unspoken rule by asking such a direct question. To cover the awkward moment she opened her handbag and groped for her cigarette case. A small metal object tinkled to the floor.

Instantly a middle-aged Italian who had been standing at the bar contemplating Diana with undisguised admiration started forward, stooped swiftly and with an elaborate bow handed the object to her.

'Thank you very much. *Grazie.*'

'*Prego, signora. Il piacere è mio.*'

With a smile which promised eternal devotion he returned to his place at the bar, from where he continued his scrutiny, this time with a faint hint of proprietorship.

Diana was staring at the small key in her hand.

'Oh, my goodness! I'd forgotten all about this.'

'What is it?'

'It's a key of some kind. Mrs Rayburn was terribly worried about what to do with it, so I said I'd hand it in to the Lost Property Office.

'You mean it didn't belong to her?'

'No, she'd found it in her bag or somewhere, and was pathetically anxious to do the right thing about it. I meant to hand it in after that meal we had but the sudden announcement about our departure put it right out of my head. Now I feel that I've let her down. The fact that she got left behind makes it somehow worse.'

'There's nothing you can do about it now. You can hand it in when we get back to Gatwick.'

'But suppose I lose it? I'm always losing things. You saw how I dropped it out of my bag.' She gave him an appealing look and he was struck again by how very expressive her eyes were. 'You wouldn't be an angel and take charge of it for me?'

'If that makes me an angel,' he said with a smile, 'I'll be only too glad.'

He took the key from her and turned it over in his hand. It had the word Sablok engraved on it and the number 28 stamped on a metal disc attached to it. He put it carefully away in one of the small fob pockets he always had fitted below the waistband of his trousers. Ten minutes later, during which time they both stuck carefully to trivialities, he put enough money on the table to cover the amount on the chit.

They had just enough time to go up to their respective rooms before the afternoon tour was scheduled to begin. When Ken came down in the lift he found Diana waiting for him near the doors.

'Ken.' She spoke quietly, glancing round to see that none of the others could hear. 'Someone's been in my room. It must have been during lunch or while we were out having coffee.'

'Well, I expect the staff have pass-keys –'

'No. I mean they've been through all my things. Everything's been left quite tidy but I can see that all sorts of small objects have been moved slightly.'

'Anything missing?'

'Not that I can see. But I never leave anything of value in a hotel bedroom any more.'

'Perhaps some misguided maid was trying to tidy up.

All the same, I think you should report this to the management.'

Diana glanced towards the group which was assembling near the hotel entrance. Gabriella was already counting heads and checking names on her list.

'Looks as if it'll have to wait until we come back from the Accademia –'

'I think this ought to be dealt with straight away and I also think it would be better if I handled it for you. You go on. I'll catch up with you.'

'But you'll miss the motor launch,' Diana pointed out, though he could see she was grateful to him for taking charge of the problem.

'I'll hire a lagonda – I mean a gondola,' he reassured her. 'The Accademia is not far. I don't think this ought to wait.'

The manager was on the defensive from the start. Though he was already running to fat his face showed him to be in his early thirties. Probably some rich uncle had helped him to secure his present position, on the basis of his sketchy knowledge of English.

'You are suggesting that one member of my personnel is not honest?'

'I'm not suggesting anything,' Ken said reasonably. 'I'm simply reporting something which I think you ought to know about.'

'You say that nothing was stolen, that there was no robbery.' The manager's hand, heavily stained with nicotine, was rotating an expensive ball-point pen.

'Apparently not. Nevertheless the lady's room was entered. Perhaps wisely she had her money and valuables on her.'

'It is not possible that an intruder should penetrate into the hotel without that someone is seeing him,' the manager declared doggedly. 'The entrance is supervised constantly though you may not perceive it. So, if one entered the room of the signora, he was a person already in the hotel, perhaps one of your own party. The door, was it locked?'

'Yes. But although your front entrance may be under constant observation the board where all the room keys are hung is not. Someone could easily have made a deliberate mistake.'

'Not so easily.' The manager drew a writing block towards him. 'We have our ways of knowing. I will notify my personnel of what has happened, but if there has been no theft I cannot call in the police.'

'We don't want you to,' Ken said placatingly. 'It's just that we thought you ought to know.'

'Thank you,' the manager said without sincerity. Ken left him conscientiously scribbling on his pad.

Instead of hiring a gondola Ken decided to take Gabriella's tip and practise the art of walking. Although the air was very hot under the still high sun, the narrowness of the streets provided plenty of shade and the constant nearness of water gave an impression of coolness. There was a fascination in walking through busy streets, hearing the murmur of a great city unadulterated by the constant fussing of motor traffic. Here the sound of footsteps, the chatter of people's voices provided a more human and reassuring background, punctuated by the occasional shout of a gondolier negotiating a tricky bend in one of the narrow canals.

He soon began to appreciate what Gabriella had said about walking being an art for Venetians, particularly the women. They carried themselves with natural grace, achieving a movement of the hips which could be as seductive as a fan dance. He found particular pleasure in watching the girls as they mounted the flights of steps that led up on to most of the bridges.

All the time he was working his way in the direction of the Accademia, checking the landmarks he had noted on the map in the hotel foyer as he passed them – Campo Santa Maria del Giglio, San Maurizio, Santo Stefano. He had to ask his way once from a postman, whose method of delivering letters was to holler at the windows above and wait for a basket to be let down on a string.

'Round the corner of San Vitale and you'll see the wooden bridge in front of you,' the postman told him, pointing.

The Gran Canale was busy with traffic at this hour and fulfilling its role as the main thoroughfare of the city. A huge barge chuffed slowly past, laden with garbage collected from hotels and houses that morning. The *vaporetto*, a water bus, was plodding up the waterway, tacking to and fro as it visited the stops on either side. Now and then one of the leaner *motoscafi* slid by, bound for the railway station or the Piazzale Roma.

And always there were the gondolas, riding the waves created by the motorized craft, the gondoliers balanced on the stern, red bands streaming from their hats, performing that mysterious punching and twisting movement which imparts to even an old man of seventy the grace of a ballet dancer.

There were flower-sellers and magazine stalls near the end of the bridge. He hesitated, ignoring the blandishments of the flower-seller, before rejecting the absurd notion of buying a rose for Diana. But a copy of the *Daily Post* on the front of the magazine stand caught his eye and to his surprise he found that it was today's.

He bought a copy, and standing there in the sunlight, turned to the financial pages to see whether the Managed Bonds into which he had put most of his money were doing any better. They weren't. They were still going down.

He refolded the paper and was about to shove it disgustedly into a refuse bin when a headline on the front page caught his eye.

'Strangled youth had been bound and whipped.'

Feeling unaccountably ashamed that the crude words had aroused his curiosity, he began to read the item.

'Police broke into a bedroom of the Crown Hotel in Earl's Court yesterday morning to find the unclothed body of a young man in bed. He had been dead for some hours.

His wrists and ankles were bound with nylon cord and he
had been gagged with sticking plaster. The body was
disfigured by weals from a lash or whip. The police doctor's
report stated that they had been inflicted before he was
strangled – '

Ken crumpled the paper before he could read any more.
Why did they have to print these details? Most normal
people would recoil in horror but there might just possibly
be others whose ghoulish curiosity would be aroused and
who would be excited to do the same.

He crossed the wooden bridge and found himself at
the Accademia di Belle Arti. Yet even here there was no
escape from violence and sublimated sadism. The composition and colouring of the canvases which adorned the wall
were aesthetically beautiful, yet so often they depicted scenes
of bestial violence. The martyrdom of Saint Sebastian tied
naked to the tree, his superb young man's torso riddled by
arrows; the fragile body of St Catherine ripped open by
the saw-toothed wheel; St Agatha with her severed breast
displayed on a dish; the ageing St Peter fastened upside
down to his cross. How could humanitarian people contemplate with apparent ecstasy such scenes of naked cruelty
and suffering? Was it because these scenes satisfied some
deep need for violence, some fascination for pain?

'You don't seem to be enjoying this very much.'

Ken spun round. Diana had walked up quietly behind
him and was looking over his shoulder at a splendid canvas
depicting the livid form of Christ nailed to the cross, flanked
by the two thieves who had been roped to their trees in
attitudes of contorted agony.

'I'm suddenly seeing this with new eyes.' He knew that
this was something he could not easily explain. 'These
pictures may be great art but I find them repellent. I'd
almost rather watch a horror film from the Hammer Film
Studios.'

'That's rather an extreme view.' Diana's comment was
quiet, but she was studying his expression with curiosity.

She had been astonished by the vehemence of Ken's out-
burst. 'What on earth has been happening to you since
I left you at the hotel?'

'Nothing,' Ken muttered. 'Just something I chanced to
see. Have you also abandoned the guided tour?'

'I came back to see if you'd found your way here. The
last time I saw them they were contemplating the Life of
St Ursula by Carpaccio.'

'If her life wound up the way I suspect it did then I don't
want to see it. Come on, let's try and find some good honest
Madonnas or Views of Venice by Canaletto and Guardi.'

'I think they're mostly in the Palazzo Rezzonico, and
that's not on our programme.'

'Then to the Palazzo Rezzonico we shall go. It's only one
stop up on the *vaporetto*.'

'Isn't that rather anti-social?'

'We can be as social as we like tonight when the culture
vultures gather for dinner.'

'Do you know, I think this is the most perfect means of
conveyance ever invented.'

Ken and Diana were sitting on the plushily-cushioned
seats of a gondola, being wafted peaceably down the Gran
Canale by a remarkably handsome and muscular *gondoliere*.
Ken's mood of repugnance had been dissipated by the
exquisite Guardis in the Ca' Rezzonico.

'Yes,' Ken agreed. 'I think that if I had to choose a time
and place in the past where I would like to have lived I'd
go for *il settecento Veneziano*.'

'You think it would be preferable to the kind of life you
live – ' Diana bit off her sentence, remembering just in
time not to make the same mistake as before.

'No, it's all right,' Ken said, laughing. 'I'm sorry if I
seemed to be choking you off that other time. The fact is
it's rather a depressing story. You see, I did have a business
of my own. De Ville Tours we called it. Had half a dozen
vintage Rolls-Royces which we kept in superb condition.

We used to convey parties of Americans round the country houses of England at vast expense. I tried to keep it going after Gillian died but the excitement had gone out of it, and it was becoming more and more expensive to keep the cars in mint condition. So when I was offered what I thought was a very good price for the business, including the site on the Fulham Road and the Rollses, I accepted. Later I discovered that the cars had been auctioned for three times the valuation I put on them and the site had been sold to a property developer for a small fortune. It's an office block now.'

'So what did you do then?'

'I took up car racing and rallying. The money I'd been paid gave me enough to finance myself. I wanted something that was exciting and dangerous enough to make me forget and frankly I didn't mind if I killed myself. In fact I did crash – pretty badly. Unfortunately I came out of it alive.'

'Don't say unfortunately.'

'You haven't heard it all. I was trapped upside down in a burning car. It was – Well, those few minutes made an indelible impression on my mind. When they let me out of hospital I found I had some kind of phobia. If I sat behind the controls of a car I became completely incapable of movement, unable to make my limbs touch the gear lever, ignition key, pedals and certainly not the steering wheel. Whenever I tried I broke into a cold sweat. The doctors warned me not to persist with it or I'd provoke a total breakdown.'

'So now you can't even drive on public roads?'

'No. Pathetic, isn't it? Luckily I have enough income to live on. I hadn't the heart to try and start up the business again. And if I get bored I can always come on a package tour, can't I?'

He finished the brief autobiography with a self-deprecatory laugh. Diana did not smile.

'It seems an awful waste to me. A man like you. You've got years before you. You should be doing something big, especially with your languages.'

'Oh, my languages don't amount to much. I've thought of trying various things but there's so little incentive these days to use any enterprise. If you rely on other people they let you down and if you operate on your own you get squeezed out by the big boys.'

'And do you still live in Fulham?'

'I have a flat in Putney. It's handy for shops and I can get into London quickly –'

'That's quite a coincidence. My former husband has bought a house in Wimbledon. That's almost on your doorstep.'

The gondola bounced gently on the bow waves of a passing launch.

'He's married again?' Ken asked cautiously.

'Oh yes,' Diana said with forced brightness. 'He's fixed up very nicely, thank you. In fact he was fixed up long before we were divorced.'

'He can't have very good taste,' Ken said, glancing at her profile. Sitting like this they were both facing the same way. It made it easier to exchange confidences somehow than being eyeball to eyeball.

'Am I to take that as a compliment?' She had turned to study the expression on his face.

'You are,' Ken said sincerely. 'You must know that you are an extraordinarily attractive woman.'

'For those who like them on the older side.' Diana spoke bitterly.

'Absolute nonsense!' Ken exploded. 'You're in the prime of a woman's life.'

Diana, pleased despite herself, gazed thoughtfully at the dome of the Salute church.

'I suppose getting divorced does something dreadful to one's self-esteem, especially when you know that your husband is going straight into some other woman's arms. Still, I don't really blame him. There's more to marriage than bed and I think we'd grown away from each other these last few years.'

A shadow passed across them and for a moment the air was cooler as they glided under a stone bridge.

'How long were you married?'

'Fourteen years,' Diana said in an incredulous voice. 'It's hard to believe, isn't it? We were far too young, of course. Our personalities had not really developed and when they did develop we found we were incompatible.'

Ken hesitated a moment before asking his next question.

'Was it a deliberate decision not to have children?'

'No. Not deliberate, though we put it off until Henry was settled in his job. Then the children just didn't come – '

'There's a lot they can do about that nowadays. Did you never consider – ?'

'We never had any tests done, if that's what you mean,' Diana cut in, with a slight hardening of her tone. 'If one of us was to blame it seemed better not to know – though it's usually the woman who has to take the blame in these cases.'

The gondola was swinging into the narrow canal where the Hotel Ruffino was situated. They both fell silent, each conscious that once again they had been ready to discuss their most private affairs on the basis of the briefest acquaintance. Ken was very aware of the physical presence of the woman beside him. He could feel that quickening in his own body which he knew as a certain sign that his companion was sexually interested. But he would have to play this very, very carefully. She was brittle and tender, still smarting from recent hurts. She might be hungry for sexual satisfaction but she would fiercely resent any assumption that, in her present situation, she was 'available'.

When Ken came down to breakfast next morning Diana was already there, but the four at the table where she was sitting was completed by Mrs Hayward and Mrs Sloman and the bat-eared Mr Tasker.

Just as well, Ken thought. They'd sat together at dinner

and people were beginning to whisper.

Miss Wilkins, the attractive but, for him, rather young physiotherapist, was sitting at a table with Mr and Mrs Grant. The seat beside her was vacant and the waiter motioned him towards it.

'Aren't you keeping this for your friend?' Ken asked the girl.

She glanced round, bit her lip and shook her head.

'Miss Norman has been taken ill,' Mrs Grant told Ken in a hushed voice as he took the seat. 'They've had to send for the doctor.'

'It's as serious as that, is it?'

'It was terrible last night,' Doreen Wilkins burst out. 'She must have vomited twenty times. I thought, you know, it's the usual gyppy tummy you hear so much about, something she'd eaten that disagreed with her, but by this morning I was convinced that she's got stomach poisoning. I wanted to get help but you try persuading a Venetian doctor to turn out at five a.m. It's obvious they've got no National Health Service here.'

'But the doctor *is* coming, isn't he, dear?'

Doreen nodded at the motherly Mrs Grant. 'She's quieter now. When I left her she was asleep. But I wish he'd hurry up. I don't like the way she's breathing.'

'You didn't eat any fish or anything funny like that? I don't always trust their fish, especially the shell-fish.'

'No, all we had, apart from what everybody else has been eating, was some ice-cream. I know ice-cream can be dangerous if the water used to make it is not pure.'

'Like as not it was the ice-cream, then.' Mr Grant, dapper this morning in a zip-front clover cardigan with dimity white edging on the collar, breast pocket and hem, nodded wisely. The top of his bald head was already beginning to peel from the hot Venetian sun. 'Probably made from water scooped out of the Grand Canal.'

Ken, who was at that moment pouring out a murky-looking cup of coffee, tried not to think of some of the objects he had seen floating in the waters of the canal.

Later, when he had gone up to his room, he was drawn to the balcony by the sound of excited conversation at the waterside below. He leant across the rail to see something which was entirely unexpected. It was a water ambulance, a motor launch equipped with a cabin exactly like the interior of a conventional ambulance, with the red cross painted on its sides and roof.

He watched as an elderly and distinguished-looking man, presumably the doctor, supervised the loading of a stretcher which had been carried out from the hotel. He caught a glimpse of the face of Alice Norman as the stretcher was placed on the rails which would slide it into the interior. The eyes were closed and her cheeks were a dirty white against the brilliance of the pillow.

Doreen Wilkins, clutching a suitcase, stepped on to the launch after her and ducked to enter the small compartment. The driver started up his engine, foam churned at the stern and the water ambulance moved towards the Grand Canal, its siren echoing eerily from the mute façades of the Byzantine and Renaissance palaces.

As Ken went down to join the party assembling for the morning's sight-seeing he found himself in the lift with Jim and Jean. As always, they were clinging close together in a half protective, half defiant way. Both wore their standard blue denim outfits. The girl had a flower patch sewn on one well-rounded buttock and on the other an inscription which read 'Look on the bright side'. They were surrounded by a pungent aura suggesting a blend of cheap eau-de-Cologne and joss sticks.

'Enjoying the tour?' Ken asked them in an endeavour to break through the intangible barrier.

'Yes, it's super,' the young man said, brushing back a lock of his long, blond hair. 'You don't really appreciate these old masters till you see the actual work on the walls. I mean, just think of the sheer physical labour of executing

those frescoes in the Palazzo Ducale. Tintoretto must have
had fantastic stamina.'

'Yes, he must.' Ken was a little taken aback by Jim's
eloquent reply. The voice was pleasant too, rather cosy and
confiding. 'You're not a painter yourself, by any chance?'

'Well, I do paint a bit.'

'Jim's a professional.' The girl squeezed his arm and
looked up into his face admiringly. 'He's really good but
it's just that he hasn't been recognized yet.'

Ken smiled. If Jim was an artist he could see why he'd
chosen this girl. She had the generous full figure which
artists prefer for nude studies.

'Jean sees my work through rose-tinted spectacles,' Jim
said modestly. 'You needn't pay any attention to her.'

'Jim and Jean,' Ken repeated the names. 'I'm Ken –
Ken Forsythe. I'd like to hear some more about a modern
painter's impressions of these old masters when there's time.'

'You're coming on the tour this morning, aren't you?'

'Well, I was a bit dubious about it,' Ken admitted. The
tour programme offered a choice for the last morning in
Venice, with the alternative of a visit to the Lido.

'You can't want to go to the Lido,' Jim protested. 'It's
a vulgar contradiction of everything that the real Venice
stands for. Whereas the Scuola San Rocco should be really
something. Tintoretto again.'

The lift had reached the ground floor and the doors were
opening.

'Perhaps I'll take your advice,' Ken said, standing back
to let Jean pass. She was wearing nothing under her denim
jacket, which was unbuttoned half way to the waist revealing the swell of a pair of unashamedly abundant breasts.

Ken followed them thoughtfully, reflecting how very
wrong you could be about people if you judged only by
external appearances.

Faced by the prospect of another dose of art appreciation
when they arrived in Padua that evening, the Grants and
the Joneses had opted for the Lido. The Prestons, in defer-

ence to the candidly expressed views of their children, had also decided in favour of the beach, and Mr Tasker was making preparations to capture some stupendous views of Venice from out on the lagoon.

So it was a select handful of eight or so who embarked with Gabriella on the launch which was to convey them up the canal. Ken took the seat beside Diana which had been tactfully left vacant by the others. They did not talk much, mainly because there was so much to look at. Gabriella's voice, on a muted loudspeaker, named the famous palaces they passed – Palazzo Gritti, Palazzo Corner, Palazzo Rezzonico, Palazzo Grimani . . .

They passed under the Ponte Rialto with its ornate balustrade and its arches enclosing the double row of small shops. At the Ca' d'Oro they disembarked and were able, under Gabriella's skilful guidance, to reconstruct in their mind's eye some idea of the munificent style of life of a Venetian patrician in the fifteenth century.

Diana had wandered off to contemplate a Venus by Titian. Following Jim and Jean, Ken found himself confronted by a Scourging, depicted by Signorelli. Still affected by the newspaper report he had read the day before, he averted his eyes quickly and began to move on.

'That sort of thing does not appeal to you?' Benson suggested blandly over his shoulder.

'No. But there's no escape, is there? Violence is thrust at you in any collection of religious paintings.'

'But it is an essential part of the whole, is it not? If there were no violence, no cruelty, there would be no martyrs. Without Judas and Pilate there would have been no Crucifixion. And if there had been no Crucifixion could there have been any Resurrection? And without Resurrection we are all damned – eternally damned.'

Ken blinked, mentally rocked by punches of such metaphysical force.

'That's as good as saying that Judas and Pilate deserve our gratitude as much as – well, the other eleven Apostles.'

E

'And why not?' Benson asked in his quiet academic voice. 'Evil is a necessary foil for Good. Without Evil there can be no Good.'

'You make virtue sound rather pointless.'

'Oh no! It gives all the more point to virtue. The contrast, the contention, the struggle is what counts. The clash of opposing forces. Without that what would be the point of our existence? I challenge you to look at that picture, to look at it frankly and honestly.'

Ken reluctantly contemplated the scene of horrific violence.

'By his stripes we are saved,' quoted Benson, his breath not improved by the day in Venice. 'The Roman soldiers are depicted as bestial, but in an indirect way they too are our saviours.'

'I can't agree with you,' Ken said shortly and moved on to join the main body of the party. For the rest of the morning he carefully avoided any risk of being cornered again by Benson.

When the party began to move on from the statue of Bartolomeo Colleoni on his charger he said to Diana: 'I've had enough. Do you feel like walking back to the hotel? We could have a drink on the way.'

'There's still the Scuola San Rocco. Don't you want to see that?'

'I'm off religion this morning. What I most want to do is pay lip service to a really cool Campari soda.'

'The Campari soda sounds tempting, but I don't want to miss those Tintorettos. If you want to go off on your own I'll tell Gabriella that you haven't fallen into the Grand Canal.'

'Thanks,' Ken said, trying not to show his disappointment. What he had really wanted was to get some time alone with Diana, but he could not very well change his mind now.

He nonetheless spent an enjoyable hour poking round the narrow *calli*, following the small, winding canals which honeycombed the city and took him away from the routes tramped by the main armies of tourists. In one café where he stopped for a drink he paid 1000 lire to have his character analysed by an expert in calligraphy, who invited him to write a few lines and then provided him with a closely-written page on the secrets of his personality.

In the end he was the last to arrive back at the hotel. Both parties had returned and were already at lunch.

He saw Gabriella talking to the manager at the reception counter and went over to have a word with her.

'Any news of that girl they took away in the ambulance this morning – Miss Norman, isn't it?'

Gabriella turned a worried face to him.

'Very bad news, I'm afraid. She's seriously ill. It sounds like a very acute case of stomach poisoning. Her friend is still with her. I'm afraid we shall just have to go on without them. I don't like doing it but we've no choice. The rooms here are booked for only two nights and we have to be in Padua by this evening.'

'Is there anything one can do?'

'Not really, thanks very much. I've notified the Consulate and she's in a very good clinic. Luckily her friend knows something about nursing.'

'This hasn't been a very lucky tour for you, has it?'

'It certainly hasn't.' Gabriella moved away with Ken as he made towards the dining-room. She felt she simply must unburden herself to someone and this mature, sympathetic man somehow invited confidence. 'And that's not all. I've just had a very worrying message from our Tours Manager at Gatwick.'

'Oh, what's happened now?'

'Well –' Gabriella hesitated. 'You remember that Mrs Rayburn we had to leave behind? I didn't want to alarm everybody but the fact is that after we took off she'd completely disappeared. We thought she must have changed her mind and gone back home. But she hasn't turned up there and she's now officially listed as a Missing Person.'

CHAPTER IV

THE COACH was waiting for the party when they arrived by *motoscafo* at the Piazzale Roma in the middle of the afternoon. Joe had acquired from the Italians his pride in the vehicle which he drove and for which he was responsible. In a sense the care and attention which he lavished on it had given him a proprietary attitude towards the compact, turquoise-blue coach. He had come to regard it as his own and would have stared uncomprehendingly at anyone who tried to explain to him that it was in reality the property of Connoisseur Tours.

In fact the vehicle was something rather special. It had been built to the order of the tour company by the Belgian firm of Van Hool. It was mounted on a Fiat chassis, powered by the 200 horsepower type 8200.12 engine. The six cylinders with their ten-litre cubic capacity had a compression ratio of 17 to 1 and were fed by direct injection. The five-speed gearbox, combined with a high-gear differential, enabled the coach to reach speeds of up to 90 m.p.h. on motorways. The steering as well as the brakes were servo assisted.

From the seat of 'the Captain', Joe presided over a dashboard that would not have disgraced an executive limousine. To his left was a console whose switches controlled the coach's lighting and air-conditioning system. The main body of the vehicle behind him was designed to provide something better than aircraft comfort for passengers who might have to face long motorway journeys. Each seat was individually adjustable to a semi-reclining position and equipped with its own ventilation and lighting switches. Broad panoramic windows were fitted with curtains which could be drawn across when the sun became too fierce. There was even a toilet at the rear with hand-basin, razor socket and flushing lavatory.

Joe had spent two hours cleaning and polishing, checking tyre pressures, oil and water levels. He had been round every seat, making sure that the control system was working properly. Now, dressed in his immaculately laundered Connoisseur blue shirt and trousers, he saw his passengers aboard with his habitual manner of mingled deference and pride. Then he carefully stowed the luggage away in the big compartment beneath the central seats. He made sure the passenger door was shut before climbing into the driver's seat.

Gabriella occupied the single front seat on his right and even when he had his eyes on the road Joe could see her trim, blue-clad form out of the corner of his eye. Joe made no secret of his admiration for Gabriella's attractions and he allowed his eyes to show it. But he had never made a pass at her. The commitment would have been too permanent and permanence was provided by Maria, his homely and chubby Triestine wife. The one-night affairs with his girl-friends in the cities of the tour gave him the release and variety which enabled him to be such a model husband and father during the periods when he was at home.

He glanced round enquiringly at Gabriella. She had removed the jacket of her uniform and the thin shirt was tight against her bosom. He thought that one deep breath might very well make the buttons pop loose. Her nipples, prodding at the material, were placed just where he liked them, set high on firm breasts.

'Is this your whole party? There were nineteen coming in to Venice and now you're down to seventeen. Where are the two girls who were sitting in the third seat near side?'

'One of them's been taken ill,' Gabriella told him in a low voice, 'and her friend's decided to stay with her.'

Joe met Gabriella's eye for a moment and nodded. He had got the message that she didn't want to discuss this in the hearing of the passengers. He started the already warm engine, checked his mirrors and eased out on to the dual carriageway that led to the mainland.

The run to Padua was a mere thirty-seven kilometres and could be easily completed in half an hour. Once on the A4 Joe let his speed build up gradually so that his passengers would not notice and soon the coach was humming along at 125 kilometres an hour, about 80 m.p.h. From his high seat Joe had a magnificent view, not so much of the countryside all around as of the traffic near him on the road, whose behaviour he studied with the concentrated attention of a formula-one racing driver. It was Joe's proud record that in seventeen years of driving coaches he had never once 'touched paint'.

Twenty-eight minutes after leaving the Piazzale Roma the coach drew up smoothly outside the Albergo Verdi in Padua, which stood between the *canale* and the Cathedral, a stone's throw from the Botanical Gardens.

The day was still young enough to allow time for another stint of sight-seeing. Gabriella and Joe had done this tour a good many times now and they had the drill efficiently worked out. Joe would be left to supervise the unloading of the suitcases from the big luggage compartment. The hotel staff would sort it out and take it up to the guests' respective rooms. Meanwhile those who were interested in cathedrals could accompany Gabriella on foot to the Basilica di Sant'Antonio.

'Do you think it's worth it?' Mrs Jones asked, as the party was descending from the coach.

'Oh, you must!' Mrs Grant exclaimed. 'I'm not a Roman Catholic but I'm a firm believer in the powers of St Anthony.'

Jean, who had overheard the conversation, looked round at Mrs Grant as if she were seeing her for the first time. 'What's he supposed to do?'

'He helps you find what you have lost,' Mrs Grant said with defensive seriousness. She was already regretting her impulsive declaration but was obstinately prepared to defend it.

'You mean,' Gareth Jones interposed in the voice he

used for making jokes, 'if I lost a golf ball in the sand-hills at Aberdovey he'd find it for me?'

Mrs Grant looked at him seriously and without anger. 'It would depend on the spirit in which you asked, Gareth. If it means a lot to you and you sincerely long to find it, then no object is too small.' She paused for a moment, then added quietly : 'And none too big.'

An odd little silence fell on the group who were listening. It was broken by Jim Collins.

'Isn't he the rather soppy-looking saint carrying the child Jesus in one hand and a lily in the other?'

'He's often shown like that, but in fact he was strong and fearless. They used to call him "the hammer of the heretics".'

'Then he'd soon hammer me,' Gareth Jones declared with his rich, stomachy laugh.

'I didn't know you were an expert on St Anthony, Mum,' Mr Grant said deprecatingly. He didn't really like 'Mum' drawing attention to herself over such a delicate matter.

'Well, I owe him a good deal.' Mrs Grant smiled round the group, trying to bring some levity into a conversation which was becoming too intense. 'At least one diamond ring, a couple of brooches, Dad's gold watch and I don't know how many other bits and pieces.'

Ken, standing on the fringes of the group, noticed that Miss Foxell had pushed closer and was listening intently to the conversation. The cooling evening air had brought up goose-pimples on her matchstick-thin, brown arms.

The result of Mrs Grant's declaration was that almost the entire party followed the blue uniform of Gabriella as she led the way towards the soaring domes, bell-towers and spires of the Romanesque Gothic building. Ken was close behind her as she entered the cathedral. He saw her dip her fingers in the font of holy water, cross herself and execute a graceful genuflection. The others, feeling slightly heathen by comparison, drifted into the shadowy, solemn interior as if under the influence of a strange hypnosis. Mrs Hayward

and Mrs Sloman draped the woollen cardigans they had
brought over their shoulders. Alan Tasker headed for the
high altar to try and photograph the sculptures of Donatello. Miss Foxell hung back and waited till the others had
moved on before purchasing a votive candle from the stall
near the entrance.

The faint tang of incense, the clusters of steadily burning
candles round the images of the Madonna, the shuffle of
unseen feet, the muted echo of voices, the colour-filtered
light from the stained glass windows, the soaring architecture – all conspired to give Ken a disturbing sense of being
in the presence of a mystery.

Gabriella's talk in the coach had primed him about what
he ought to see, but for ten minutes he just wandered at
random round the great building, staring up into the gloom
of the vaulted ceiling, gazing at the frescoes, peering into
side chapels where occasional little groups of anonymous
worshippers knelt in prayer.

He was standing in front of the black Donatello sculptures adorning the high altar when he heard a light step
behind him.

'Have you seen the tomb of the saint?' It was the gentle
voice of Gabriella, close to his ear.

He turned and looked down into her face. The expression
of hushed reverence made her intensely attractive and only
the provocatively slanted tambourine hat prevented her
from resembling one of Botticelli's more delightful female
martyrs.

Ken restrained lascivious thoughts and admitted that he
had not realized the saint was buried inside the cathedral.

'But, of course,' she said, shaking her head reprovingly
at this inattentive pupil who had not listened carefully
enough to her talk in the bus. 'That is why they built the
Basilica. The tomb is in the Capella dell'Arca, to the left
of the high altar there. You should not miss it.'

'I won't. I promise you.'

She smiled forgiveness, her lips moving against each

other in a way which showed that she had guessed the nature of his thoughts. Not for the first time Ken wondered why churches make attractive women look so much more sexy.

He moved in the direction she had indicated, found the elaborately decorated chapel with the tomb in the middle. A narrow corridor led round behind the tomb itself, which was enclosed within marble slabs. At the back, where visitors were able to pass closest to the saint's body, the marble had, over the centuries, been polished smooth and shiny by the supplicant hands, cheeks or lips of countless pilgrims.

As he rounded the corner he saw to his acute embarrassment that he had invaded a moment of privacy. A woman was standing there, her body and forehead pressed against the marble. The outspread fingers of both hands were laid flat on the cold stone. Her eyes were closed. Uncontrollable sobs racked her body.

Ken stopped, not knowing what to do. He remembered Mrs Grant's words. 'No object is too small. And none too big.' With a shock he realized that the biggest loss you can suffer is that of a human being, a human life. He knew for certain that the academic, the earnest, the desiccated Miss Foxell had come to beg for the return of someone she had loved – and lost.

Enough time passed for a burnt-out candle to splutter and die. Then she opened her eyes and saw him. She twisted away and stumbled out of the dark little passage.

He waited there for a few minutes, running his hand over the smooth surface. No miracle could ever return to him the person he had lost and he formulated no wish or prayer. If there really was a power within this marble perhaps it would sense the void in his life and send something to fill it.

When he emerged from the Capella dell'Arca it was to be confronted with yet another of those insights which completely altered his whole judgement of a person's character. Blinded by her tears, Miss Foxell had stumbled upon, of all people, the trenchant, keep-your-distance Mrs Hayward. And Mrs Hayward had Miss Foxell's head on her breast. Her arms were round the thin, shaking shoulders. She was patting her gently and in her deep, almost masculine voice was murmuring the kind of fundamental reassurances you give to a small, frightened child.

Ken slipped past and made for the exit. As he emerged the evening sunlight blazed at him. He blinked and shook his head as if to clear it after a long, underwater dive. Diana was waiting with the rest of the party who had collected outside the arched doorway. When she saw his face she came over to him.

'Ken. Are you all right? You look as white as a ghost.'

'Yes, I'm perfectly all right. Just something I saw in there shook me a bit.'

She wanted to ask him more but bit back the questions when she saw the warning in his eyes.

'Mr Forsythe,' Gabriella called over to him. 'Do you know if Mrs Hayward and Miss Foxell are still in the building?'

Ken nodded. 'Yes. They are. But don't wait for them. I think they want to look around for a little longer.'

Gabriella consulted her watch and shrugged.

'Well, I think we must move on if we are going to see the Botanical Gardens.'

'Ah!' Gareth Jones remarked with satisfaction. 'Now that's something a bit more in my line of country.'

'The Botanical Gardens of Padua,' Gabriella began in her courier's voice, 'are among the oldest in Europe and are unparalleled for the variety and rarity of their specimens –'

Ken liked flowers but their names always baffled him and he had given up any attempt at memorizing them. As they went through the gardens he drifted along at the back of the group, admiring the movement of Gabriella's behind as she walked, comparing her slim svelteness with the pneumatic promise of Diana's more mature and manageable body. The latter, he could see, was something of an expert on horticulture and constantly stooped to examine the name-tags attached to the rarer plants.

Miss Foxell and Mrs Hayward had not rejoined the party by the time they returned to the hotel. All the suit-cases had been spirited away from the entrance hall and Gabriella had disappeared to change out of her daytime uniform into her evening outfit. Ken walked over to the reception desk to find out the number of the room he had been allocated. He had to wait patiently while the clerk tried to explain to a rather illiterate but very pig-headed Sicilian that full pension terms only applied to stays of more than three days.

'You are in number 75 on the third floor, signore,' the clerk was telling Ken when the lift doors opened and the squat figure of Gareth Jones in braces erupted from them. His face was scarlet with indignation.

'What the devil have you people done with our suitcases?' he demanded, ignoring the fact that the clerk was talking to Ken.

'Excuse me, signore. I do not understand.'

'Our suitcases, man. I saw them being taken from the bus and put in the hall and they were supposed to be taken up to our rooms – '

'You have looked in your room, signore?' The clerk collected his wits and rapidly consulted a list. 'Your name, please?'

'Jones. Room 26.' Gareth Jones gave the information as if daring the clerk to contradict him. 'And of course we've looked in our room!'

'Yes. That is correct. Your suitcases should be there, signore.'

'Indeed they should,' Gareth Jones said with dangerous calm. 'But they are not. That is what I have come down here to tell you.'

'There must be some mistake – ' the clerk suggested, unwisely falling back on the old cliché.

'You're damn right there's some mistake!' Gareth Jones roared, his patience suddenly giving way. 'Now I want those suitcases found without delay or I promise you I shall make such a fuss with your management that –'

Ken took his key from the counter and retreated to the lift. He found that number 75 was on the second floor at the back of the hotel. He put the key in the lock, which was incorporated in the handle. When you closed the door from inside it automatically locked unless you operated a small catch. His own suitcase reposed intact on the wooden stand at the end of the bed.

He unpacked and rang Room Service for a Punt e Mes while he showered and changed. He could hear a good deal of movement in the hotel. Footsteps kept hurrying along the corridor outside, doors kept opening and closing. He had put on a clean pair of briefs and was slipping his arms into a fresh shirt when the telephone rang.

It was Gabriella, asking him if by any chance he had in his room a suitcase which was not his own.

'Sorry, no. Are they still looking for the Joneses'?'

'Yes, and to judge by the fuss he's kicking up he has the crown jewels inside.'

'Bad luck. I hope you find them soon.'

'Thanks. And Mr Forsythe. Do make sure you lock your door when you come down to dinner.'

'Yes. I usually do. But you have some special reason for saying that?'

'Yes. I'll explain later.'

She hung up rapidly, obviously in a hurry to telephone other members of her party.

Half an hour later when Ken came down in the hope of meeting Diana in the Cocktail Bar he found Gabriella surrounded by the entire Preston family. She had not even had time to change out of her day uniform. Mr Preston's moustache was bristling with indignation and his wife's brow was furrowed with motherly care. Their two offspring were jerking with suppressed excitement. They had in their eyes the expression of puppies who have come upon a half-dead rabbit and have suddenly become vicious.

'But our things were turned absolutely inside out!' Mrs Preston was complaining, as she tried to poke her wayward hair into place. 'All the suitcases had been opened and the contents strewn over the floor. It'll take us hours to tidy up.'

'Was anything stolen?' Gabriella, concerned but still outwardly calm, put the question quietly.

'How can we possibly tell?' Mr Preston said. 'You can't carry an inventory of everything you bring on holiday.'

'I mean valuables – jewellery, cameras, watches or your wallet or handbag.'

'Oh, we're not such fools as to leave real valuables in a hotel bedroom.'

'I think my camel-skin belt is missing,' Emma said. 'The one Daddy bought for me in Tunisia.'

'And I had a bone-handled flick-knife which I can't see anywhere,' Nigel added, with a certain malicious satisfaction.

'All sorts of things may be missing.' Mrs Preston put an arm protectively on her daughter's shoulder. 'But it's not only that. It's the inconvenience and knowing that someone has been pawing over your things.'

Gabriella was holding on to her calm with a great effort. Standing watching the scene, Ken reflected that she had in a way been made the victim of her own consistent politeness and courtesy. The Prestons thought they could throw anything at her but in fact she was approaching the limit of what she could take.

He caught her eye over their heads and gave her a friendly wink.

'I'm very sorry it has happened, Mr Preston, and you can be sure I shall take it up with the hotel management. If you find that anything's missing please let me know and we can decide whether to call in the police. And if it's not covered by your personal insurance policy I will see what our own insurers can do to help.'

Slightly mollified, the Prestons broke off the engagement
and, still worrying the subject among themselves, headed
towards the dining-room.

Ken strolled over to join Gabriella. She gave him a wry
smile.

'I hope you haven't come with a complaint, Mr Forsythe.'

'No. But I saw the Prestons giving you a pretty rough
ride.'

'These things never come singly.' She paused to flash a
dazzling smile at Mr Benson, who had just emerged from
the lift. 'I'm waiting for the third blow to fall.'

'Any luck with the Joneses' suitcases?'

'Yes. Thank goodness. We found them in the end. They
had been shoved into one of the linen rooms on the first
floor. The contents were in a terrible mess. Someone had
pulled all their things out and then just shoved them back
higgledy-piggledy.'

'Quite obviously there's a thief at work.'

'I know.' Gabriella's smooth brow was momentarily
wrinkled. 'The funny thing is that no one has been able
to say definitely that anything was stolen.'

She stopped, listening anxiously as the telephone on the
reception desk began to ring. The young clerk picked it up.

'*Pronto . . . Si, dica . . . Un attimo, per favore . . .*'

He took the receiver away from his ear and called to
Gabriella. 'Signorina, your call to Venezia.'

Gabriella put a hand on Ken's arm. 'That must be a
call from Miss Wilkins. I had a message to ring her. Would
you – you wouldn't come and be with me while I take it in
the manager's office?'

It would have been hard to refuse the appeal even if he
had wanted to. She spoke rapidly to the clerk in Italian and
led Ken into the manager's office. Its occupant was out and
about somewhere in the hotel, quizzing the members of
his staff in an endeavour to locate the missing master key
to all the bedrooms.

Ken closed the door and sat down on the end of the desk. Gabriella took the swivel chair behind it, pulled the telephone towards her and crossed her legs. The light nylon skirt slid back on the flesh-coloured tights she was wearing.

'*Pronto* ... Ah, Miss Wilkins. Yes. it's Gabriella speaking. How is your friend?'

Ken could hear the agitated voice on the other end of the line but he could not make out the words. He saw Gabriella's expression change.

'Oh no! ... At what time? ... Oh my dear, I am so very sorry. Were you with her when she – ?'

She glanced up at Ken and then listened for a long time.

'Yes, I do understand. But is there any real point in staying in Venice? I mean, what more can you do now, and if her parents are flying out tomorrow ... No, it's not good for you to be alone in a strange city after all you've been through. Now listen. I am coming back to fetch you ... No, I'm coming back to fetch you. It is much better for you to be with the party and if you decide to go straight home we can arrange it. Can you make your way to the Hotel Ruffino? ... I'll pick you up there. I don't know how long it will be, perhaps an hour, perhaps more ... Yes, I'm quite sure that is the best thing. Look after yourself now and see you soon.'

She put the receiver down and only then dropped her eyes from Ken's face.

'Sounds pretty bad,' he suggested.

'It is. Her friend died at about six this evening. It's so extraordinary. I didn't know stomach poisoning could kill you as quickly as that.'

Gabriella stood up and began to move round the end of the desk where he sat.

'Aren't you taking on rather a lot by going back to fetch her? You seem to have enough on your plate already.'

'It's the least I can do. I feel now I should not have left them in Venice. I just hope I can find Joe. I'll get him to drive me back in the coach.'

'You know,' Ken said, looking into the face which was now on a level with his own. 'You're a pretty wonderful person.'

Maybe it was the sudden word of kindness amid so much criticism that released the tension in Gabriella, maybe it was an instinctive need to have someone older and stronger to lean on. But suddenly her hands met at the back of his neck and her lips came slowly forward till they were in contact with his own.

He put his arms round her waist, and still half sitting, drew her close against him. Her body was pliable and responsive, he could feel the softness of her breasts against his chest.

Then, before the kiss changed gear, she broke it off and snuggled her face against the side of his neck. He could feel the wetness of tears against his skin. For a good minute he held her, feeling her heart beating against his ribs.

At last she drew away and he did not try to restrain her.

'I wish I could do something to help.'

'You have.' She had found a handkerchief and was drying her eyes. 'I needed that – a shoulder to cry on. I feel better now.'

Ken stood up, controlling the desire to seize hold of her again and take that tentative kiss a lot deeper.

'I'm coming back to Venice with you,' he said decisively.

'No, Mr Forsythe,' she shook her head vigorously. 'Joe will take me –'

'Don't you think you'd better call me Ken – after that?'

'Yes, I will call you Ken – but only when we are alone. Couriers are not supposed to flirt with the passengers.'

'Then I hope we'll be alone often. In the meantime I'd like to do something to help.'

Gabriella put a hand forward to push back a lock of his hair which had fallen over his forehead.

'There is something you could do. I think our Tours Operator ought to know about this. Mr Sampson – we call him Sammie. If I give you his home number do you think you could phone him?'

'Of course I will,' Ken said, moving to open the door for her. 'As the Italians say, *commandi, signorina.*'

Then for the first time he saw her real smile, the one that came from the heart.

'*Grazie, signore. La ringrazio assai.*'

Ken managed to finish his dessert and gulp a quick Espresso before the reception clerk came to tell him that his call to England was through.

Sampson listened in silence while Ken gave him Gabriella's message and explained that she'd gone back to Venice to collect Doreen Wilkins.

'Good girl,' he commented. 'You can always count on Gabriella.'

'She's had a very sticky tour so far,' Ken said and told Sampson about the stolen suitcase and rifled bedroom.

'That's a rum go. I wonder if we have a professional thief among our party. That's the trouble, we've no way of knowing who we're booking in on these tours. They may be somebody's maiden aunt but they could equally well be a homicidal maniac.'

'Encouraging thought,' Ken murmured. 'What was all this about poor old Mrs Rayburn?'

'How do you know about that? I explicitly told Gabriella not to make it public.'

'She didn't make it public. But the poor girl has to have someone to confide in and for reasons best known to herself she chose me. No one else knows.'

'Well, keep it under your hat. It's a police matter now and they've passed it to their Missing Persons department.'

Ken lit a small cigar and waited in the hotel foyer for Diana to come out of the dining-room. He still felt fired up after his contact with Gabriella and very much desired some female company. He had seen her sitting at a table with Jim and Jean, Alan Tasker and the ever-attentive

F

Mr Benson, and was relieved to see when she came out that she had somehow managed to shake them off.

He intercepted her as she crossed the foyer.

'*Ciao.*'

'*Ciao,*' she answered. 'You're acting very mysterious this evening. Have you been on the hot line or something?'

'I can't talk about it here. Do you feel like a *passeggiata*? It's a lovely warm night.'

She only hesitated for a moment. 'Yes, I'd like that. Just let me get a woolly from my room.'

When she came down he saw that she had renewed her make-up and there was a fragrance of Arpège about her. The woolly was a very soft and wispy shawl which she had put over her step-in shirtwaister dress.

They strolled past the Botanical Gardens to the Prato del Valle, crossed a stone bridge and entered the park enclosed by an elliptical canal in which a long line of statues was reflected. In the background the humped and spiky outline of the Basilica was outlined against a sky made luminous by the glow of the city's street lights.

Ken was trying to describe one of the Donatello sculptures when Diana suddenly said: 'Why don't you want to talk about it?'

'About what?'

'Whatever happened in the cathedral. I could see by your face when you came out you'd had a shock of some kind.'

'I saw something I shouldn't have. Someone's private grief. In a way I feel that to talk about it would be breaking a confidence.'

'I understand.' He felt her arm slip into his and he shortened his stride so that they could keep in step. 'Forgive me for being tactless.'

'It's funny how your ideas of people change. That odd assortment who gathered at Gatwick, you'd never have suspected the hidden depths – '

'I suspected hidden depths the first time I saw you, when

you were collecting your voucher. I somehow sensed then that I was going to come to know you well.'

'And I made my mind up that I was going to do something about getting to know you. I'm afraid the way I grabbed the seat beside you in the aircraft made it a bit obvious.'

'You certainly made up for it afterwards,' Diana said with feeling. 'I began to wonder if you were ever going to speak to me again.'

Ken laughed. 'It was just that I didn't want to rush you.'

'I know,' she agreed quietly. 'It is a mistake to rush things.'

They walked on for a few minutes in silence. The murmur of the city seemed remote under the shadow of the trees.

'Ken, do you think all package tours are like this?'

'In what way do you mean?'

'You know what I mean. Don't you? Is it just coincidence that Mrs Rayburn missed the plane at Gatwick and that poor little Alice Norman got herself poisoned in Venice, that my room was searched yesterday and the Prestons' today – not to mention that odd businesses with the Joneses' suitcases?'

'I've been thinking about it quite a lot. I know I can rely on you to keep this to yourself – '

'Of course.'

'Mrs Rayburn has never been seen again. She didn't return to her home and the police have listed her as a Missing Person. I only hope she's still alive.'

Diana stopped and swung round to face him. 'You think she may have had a heart attack?'

'A heart attack or some other kind of attack.'

'Who would want to attack a harmless old thing like Mrs Rayburn?' He felt through Diana's arm the shiver that ran down her body. 'You don't think there could be any connection between that and Alice Norman?'

'I don't see how. She's if anything even more harmless than Mrs Rayburn. I suppose this is just one of those unlucky tours, where everything goes wrong. Gabriella says it sometimes happens like that.'

'And all these searchings?'

'A thief – or thieves. Package tourists offer very easy pickings, you know.'

They had started to walk on. She turned round to look back down the dark path they had come along. The trees cast patches of shadow which could camouflage moving shapes.

'You're not frightened, are you?'

'No. Not with you. I thought I heard a footstep, but there's no one there. That's why a man takes a woman on his left arm, isn't it? So that his right hand is free to draw his sword.'

'So I've heard. Unfortunately I left my sword in my other suit. Seriously, though, it's hard to imagine anything sinister in the party we've got on this tour.'

'You said a moment ago that people kept showing hidden depths.'

'Yes, but I was really meaning things like Mrs Grant and her fervent belief in the powers of St Anthony, the fact that Jim with his blue Jean turns out to be an expert on painting. And Mrs Hayward looks as cold as charity, but if you'd seen her mothering Miss Foxell in the cathedral –'

Ken stopped. Diana gave his arm an impatient shake. 'Come on! You've let it out now so you may as well tell me the rest.'

'Oh, it was just that I found her sobbing her heart out against the back of the tomb.'

'She was praying for the return of something – or somebody,' Diana said thoughtfully. 'You know, I had a peculiar experience in there myself. For a moment it occurred to me to ask for my old life and the happiness Henry and I had at the beginning. And then it suddenly struck me that there is nothing that I possessed in the past that I truly want back. I shall not trouble St Anthony, not yet at any rate. Perhaps there is some other saint whose job it is to replace what was lost with something completely different, though I'm not sure that I'd ever pray to him. I believe we have to find these things for ourselves.'

They had reached the farther side of the park and met the opposite segment of the narrow waterway which enclosed it.

'Would you rather go round the outside? It's lighter.'

'No, so long as you're there I'm not frightened.'

They turned back to retrace their steps and covered a hundred yards without any other communication than the unforced contact of their bodies against each other. Then he felt Diana give a slight start. Following her gaze he saw what looked almost like a modernistic statue at the side of the path. Two figures, steely blue in the filtered light, a man and a woman fused into one form. Then the woman's head moved as she rolled it to intensify the kiss and the Titian-tinted hair caught splinters of light. The man's hand slid down across the tightly strained jeans.

If they heard Ken and Diana they did not take any notice of them.

'Jim and Jean,' Diana whispered, when they had gone on a little way. 'They don't seem to tire of it, do they?'

'Well, we're only two nights out and it's quite obvious that they're not one of your settled married couples.'

'They had a pretty wild session that first night in Venice. The Grants were in the room above and they couldn't get much sleep. Tickles and spanks, I expect. I must say that arriving in Venice by moonlight was a highly stimulating experience.'

'I've never considered before that great architecture could have an aphrodisiac effect.'

'It's not surprising, really. It's a stimulation of the senses. Sometimes I find that magnificent scenery has the same effect. After a day in the Alps I feel I want to make love all night.'

One of the most effective of aphrodisiacs, Ken was thinking, is a conversation like this one with an attractive woman. Diana's frankness, her readiness to talk about sexuality without inhibition was beginning to rouse him. The touch of her forearm on his had become the channel for an almost electric current. His mouth had gone slightly dry.

They walked on for no more than twenty yards before their hands, as if determined of their own accord to bring the matter to a head, met and interlocked, the fingers intertwining. Her grip was strong and eager. He stopped, and maintaining his imprisoning grip, twisted her round to face him.

'Diana.'

'Yes – '

They looked at each other for a moment, both very much aware that they were about to cross a great divide. Then he bent his head and put his lips, gently at first, against hers. Her mouth was moister and softer than Gabriella's. Her lips parted and he felt the first quick contact of her tongue. His hand went round her and he gripped hard, pressed her to him so that it hurt.

When they drew apart, breathing deeply to release tension, they both knew that this was not enough. There had to be more – and soon.

'Let's go back,' Diana whispered, her voice slightly husky. 'It's suddenly cold.'

They walked slightly apart, as if wary now of the force which a mere touch could unleash. The hotel was quiet as they passed through the foyer, collecting their keys from an impersonal night clerk.

'Which floor?' Ken asked, as the lift doors opened for them.

'My room's on the third. Let's go there.'

The lift thrust at their feet and then gave them a moment of weightlessness as it slowed for the third floor. Diana stepped out into the empty corridor. He walked beside her till they came level with room number 121.

No questions asked, no invitation given. She simply

handed him her key. He bent to put it in the lock, opened
the door. Then only she took his hand and drew him inside.
She did not release him till he had closed the door, which
automatically locked itself from the inside. Then she pressed
the switch which turned on the low lamp by the bedside.
She drew off her shawl and let it fall to the floor, kicked
away her shoes, and put her arms round his neck.

'Please, darling. Be quick. Don't keep me waiting.'

He had listened to the friendly clock striking three and had
just eased his leg from under one of hers when he heard a
faint sound from the direction of the door. It could have
been someone very cautiously testing the handle.

He cocked an ear, straining to listen. Beside him Diana
was still breathing steadily.

After perhaps half a minute there came a faint metallic
sound, a kind of tinkling scrape. He was sure that a key
was being inserted gently into the lock.

He pushed the sheet back and rolled out of bed. The
springs emitted a faint twang and instantly the scraping
sound stopped. On his hands and knees now, Ken crept
across the floor till he was opposite the door. By laying his
cheek on the carpet he could just see the crack of light
under it. There were two shadows cast by the legs of the
person crouching outside.

He would have liked to get some clothes on before
grappling with an intruder but he had flung them off without thinking and there was no chance of finding them in the
dark. The faint scraping sound came again.

The wardrobe stood against the wall at right angles to
the doorway. He stood up and tip-toed over to the triangle
of deeper darkness beside it. Naked or not, he intended to
find the answer to one of the mysteries of this strange
package tour – the identity of the thief who had been
pilfering from the rooms.

The intruder took infinite precautions about getting the
door open and managed to do so almost soundlessly. All at

once there was a chink of light from outside. After a few seconds it widened and a figure slipped into the room.

He closed the door as carefully as he had opened it and the room was again dark. There was barely enough light filtering through the curtains for Ken to follow his movements.

Ken waited to see what he would do, hoping that if the man turned his back he could jump him.

He moved towards the bed and Ken assumed that he was just making sure that Diana was asleep. But something about the figure's manner and the knowledge that an unknown intruder was so close to that body for which he would not now have traded the whole world started the alarm bells ringing in his mind.

'Hold it!' he said loudly.

The figure spun round and almost at the same moment he was blinded by the beam of a torch shining straight into his eyes.

And it was coming at him!

He felt incredibly vulnerable in his nakedness and had to resist a ridiculous impulse to put his hands down to protect his private parts. Instead, he charged towards the light, thrusting his hands before him in an endeavour to make contact.

The light went out and he knew that the man must duck sideways to avoid his onrush. But he was already committed and could not stop. He flung a hand out, slapped against a limb and got a grip on the thin, clingy material. That swung him round and he threshed with his free hand to get a double grip. A searing pain stabbed up his right forearm and he involuntarily loosened his grip. He recovered at once and, enraged by the pain, lunged out at the empty darkness.

'Darling! What on earth are you doing?'

Diana had woken up. He could hear her struggling clear of the bedclothes.

He shouted: 'Switch the light on!'

He heard her scrabbling at the bedside table but before she could turn the light on the door opened. He caught one more quick glimpse of the figure as it slipped out into the corridor, banging the door behind it.

He rushed to the door, but something had made the handle sticky and he could not turn it. It took him a moment to realize that it was his own blood. That brought realization that his arm was extremely painful and that in any case he could not pursue the intruder through the corridors of the hotel stark naked.

'Get that light on, for God's sake!'

Diana was still groping her way into wakefulness. She knocked a tumbler of water off the table before she at last managed to switch the light on.

She saw Ken standing in the centre of the room, blinking at the light, one hand on the wound in his arm, the blood trickling down his wrist and on to his fingers.

'My God! What on earth have you done to yourself?'

'I didn't do it to myself,' he snapped unreasonably. 'While you've been asleep we've had an intruder.'

'An intruder. You mean the thief?'

'I suppose so.'

'Did you manage to see him?'

'I'm not sure it was a man. The material I grabbed felt more like a dress, and the flesh felt – sort of squishy.'

'A woman? But that's incredible.'

'Look, do you think you could help me with this arm? It's only going to make a mess on the carpet.'

'Oh darling, I'm sorry. I'm not really awake yet and I can't believe I'm not dreaming this –'

Whilst he sat on the bathroom stool with a towel round his shoulders she bathed the long slash on his forearm, listening with intent concern to his account of the incident.

'This was done with a very sharp knife, perhaps even a razor.'

'Maybe the flick knife which the Preston boy said he'd lost,' Ken suggested. 'At any rate it seems to be a clean wound.'

'It really ought to have stitches. I'm going to telephone for a doctor as soon as I've got some sort of dressing on it. And surely we ought to notify the police.'

'And explain how I came to be standing naked in your room at three o'clock in the morning?'

'Darling, don't be so old-fashioned!' Diana laughed. 'You don't have to worry about my maidenly reputation. I'm more concerned about your arm. Here, hold this hand-kerchief against it while I find something to make a bandage out of.'

She went into the bedroom, opened a drawer and came back with a white cotton shirt from which she ripped a strip long enough to make a bandage.

'I don't fancy the idea of having myself stitched by some unknown doctor,' he said, as she bound his forearm tightly. 'Besides, whoever that blasted person was, he or she is either safely back in their own room or well away from the hotel already. It's not worth making myself the laughing-stock of the whole party –'

'Well, I just hope the knife hadn't been used for de-gutting rabbits. Tomorrow I must get some proper dressings from the chemist. You weren't able to see the face, I suppose?'

'Not really. All I could make out was some sort of light coloured material. It may have been nylon. It was very slippery to the touch. That's why I couldn't get a proper grip.'

'I suppose –' Diana tore the end of the strip of cotton so as to be able to finish off with a knot – 'it couldn't have been any member of our party?'

'It *could* have been,' Ken agreed. 'But can you see any of them breaking into a bedroom in the dead of 'ight armed with a knife?'

'Not really.' Diana finished the knot off and wiped the

bloodstained water from his arm and hand. 'There. I think
the bleeding has stopped. It could have been worse.'

'It could have been a lot worse,' Ken agreed, standing up.

She took him by the good hand and led him back into
the bedroom. Her body was tanned a deep brown except
for the area which had been covered by the lower part of a
bikini.

'Come back to bed and let me cosset you. You don't
have to go back to your room for a long time yet, do you?'

'I'm not going to leave you till it's daylight, that's for
sure. Whatever they were looking for they didn't get it, so
just in case they come back – '

There was still no sign of Diana in the dining-room when
Ken finished his own breakfast. When he came out into
the foyer he found the Joneses and the Prestons clustered
round a tired-looking Gabriella and the harassed hotel
manager. Mr Preston was very British in a blue, double-
breasted blazer with brass buttons.

'No, there's no point,' Mr Jones was saying. 'If we do
lodge an official complaint with the police we'll only be held
up for hours making statements, and if they catch the chap
they'd have to haul us back here to make the charge stick.'

'But people can't be just allowed to get away with things
like that,' Mrs Preston argued virtuously. 'It only encourages
them to try again.'

Mr Jones put a hand on the manager's shoulder, and
half closed one eye.

'I think signore here is going to take care they don't get
away with it again. He's suffered enough already, poor
chap.'

Indeed the hotel manager seemed in a mood close to
suicide. Apart from the good reputation of his hotel, he
now had to contemplate the cost of changing the locks on
all the bedroom doors.

Gabriella said, 'I think that's the best decision. Especially
as no one seems to have lost anything.'

'Except my flick-knife,' Nigel Preston pointed out.

'The less said about that the better,' his father warned him. 'They might pull you in for carrying an offensive weapon.'

'God, I never thought of that!'

'Don't say God like that,' Mrs Preston hissed in an audible whisper. 'I've told you I don't know how many times.'

Ken had seen Doreen Wilkins in the small lounge adjoining the foyer. She was standing alone, staring out of the window. He went in and at the sound of his footsteps she turned round. To his relief he saw that she was perfectly composed, though her face showed signs of the strain she had been under.

'I needn't say how sorry I am about your friend. It was a shocking thing to happen.'

'Thanks. People are being so kind to me.' She seemed to feel ill at ease in her trendy bell-bottomed trousers and jersey top with its palm-tree motif. 'Gabriella was absolutely marvellous. Did you know that she and Joe came all the way back to Venice for me in that whacking great coach?'

'Yes. She told me she was going to fetch you. I'm sure you made the right decision coming along with the tour. At times like this it's good to have company and plenty to think about.'

Doreen looked him straight in the eye with a hardening of the expression on her freckled face. The nostrils of her small, upturned nose contracted.

'Oh,' she said in a voice of suppressed passion. 'Wild horses wouldn't drag me away from the tour – not now.'

She walked past him and left him standing there contemplating the carpet.

CHAPTER V

THE LAST THING that Ken and Diana wanted was to be spotted by their fellow package tourists as another pair of lovers, though of a more mature vintage than Jim and Jean. Ken avoided being in too close company with Diana, but he constantly kept an eye on her. He could not escape from the uncomfortable thought that the person who had entered her room the night before and had stooped so menacingly over her bed must have had the knife ready, the blade opened.

The main feature of the morning's programme was the visit to the Scrovegni Chapel, which was far enough away to justify using Joe's coach. During the short trip Gabriella picked up the microphone and gave her usual introductory talk.

'The Scrovegni Chapel, sometimes known as the Arena Chapel, was built with the express purpose of receiving frescoes. And the painter chosen was Giotto, whom many consider to be the great painter of the Italian Renaissance. He carried out the work about 1305.'

Ken admired the way she was maintaining a hold on the tour, keeping the arranged programme going despite the alarming series of misfortunes.

'The thirty-eight frescoes tell the story of Mary and Jesus, and above the door is a vast work depicting the Last Judgement. This is the most complete and important cycle of Italian medieval paintings and one of the most remarkable things about them is their excellent state of preservation.'

Another Last Judgement, Ken reflected ruefully, and waited while the others descended from the coach. Miss Foxell still had her guide book to which she constantly referred and Mr Tasker was equipped with his inevitable cameras. The man Benson was trying to chat up Mrs Hay-

ward and Mrs Sloman and making very little progress.
The Grants were dutifully drinking in everything that was
offered them, though the Joneses had decided to give the
morning's tour a miss and go shopping instead. Diana, with
protective friendliness, had tacked herself on to Doreen
Wilkins and her influence had done something to break
down the girl's remote and faintly hostile manner.

Once inside the chapel Ken found that his qualms had
been quite unjustified. The sincerity and simplicity of
Giotto's paintings, the compassion which imbued every
scene of suffering quite disarmed him and he found himself
gazing with a kind of excited joy at the incredible blue and
golden tints which had remained so fresh for over six
centuries.

'It's his use of empty space that's so amazing,' Ken
heard Jim whispering to Jean. They were standing just
behind him. 'Look at that outstretched hand – and all those
staves pointing to the blue sky.'

'Jim, why have all the women got those funny eyes – sort
of Chinky?'

'It's a sort of, well, like a chorus wearing the conventional
mask of grief.'

'I like the little angels,' Jean said with a chuckle. 'And
those funny sheep and goats. But up there – is that two men
kissing each other?'

'Only one man is doing the kissing,' Jim corrected her.
'That is the Kiss of Judas.'

Owing to the matter of the ransacked room and missing
suitcases the morning's tour was running late and Gabriella
was trying to make up for some of the lost time. She
managed to shepherd most of her party out to the coach
but Alan Tasker was still dismantling his tripod and
Mrs Hayward and Mrs Sloman simply would not be hurried
over their inspection of the Pietà. Standing beside Gabriella
at the doorway, Ken tried unsuccessfully to picture either
of them entering a locked bedroom with a knife in their
hand. People might have unsuspected depths but that was

pushing credibility too far.

'I wish they'd hurry,' Gabriella said. 'We've still got the Piazza delle Erbe and the Museo Civico to see before lunch.'

'I managed to get through to your friend Sampson in the end,' Ken said in a low voice.

'I'm very grateful. We weren't back till rather late. I thought of phoning you, but decided I'd better not disturb your sleep.'

She gave him a slightly mischievous smile.

'That was thoughtful,' Ken said, wondering whether she had in fact rung his room and received no answer.

'Oh Ken, I'll be so thankful when we get away from this place. I feel I never want to see Padua again.' She put a hand on his arm and lowered her voice. 'Watch out. They're coming at last. Do you think I could see you tonight? I do want to talk to you.'

She was looking at him with an unmistakable appeal.

'We'll try and fix that,' he said. 'When we get to Verona.'

He had an odd feeling that he had been disloyal to Gabriella. The desire which she had awakened in him had precipitated and enriched his collision with Diana. Did the fact that he now wanted Gabriella as well mean that he was in some way depraved?

Joe's coach polished off the eighty kilometres of autostrada from Padua to Verona in about three-quarters of an hour. By mid-afternoon the party were standing gazing at the balcony of the Casa di Giulietta. Mrs Hayward and Mrs Sloman were engaged in one of their customary arguments.

'Of course it's a completely bogus story put out to fool the tourists,' Mrs Hayward stated firmly in her strong voice. 'There's absolutely no evidence that any such families as the Capulets and Montagues ever existed and certainly no record of any Romeo or Juliet.'

'I prefer to think otherwise,' Mrs Sloman stoutly replied. 'Why do you have to demolish everything, Nancy? Even if they didn't have the names Shakespeare gave them, I firmly believe that the characters existed.'

'I suppose you also believe that there was a Merchant of Venice who solemnly demanded his pound of flesh – or *mezzochilo*, as he should have said.'

'I don't see why not.' The two ladies were quite unaware that most of the party were now riveted on their discussion. 'After all, we know *Othello* is based on an old Venetian fable.'

'Oh, come! You'll be telling me next that you have the address and telephone number of the Two Gentlemen of Verona.'

Before Mrs Sloman could think of a retort a voice behind them intoned clearly : 'I will kiss thy lips; haply some poison yet doth hang on them.'

The heads of Mrs Hayward and Mrs Sloman turned as one. Ken did not need to look round. He had recognized the voice as that of Doreen Wilkins.

'I beg your pardon,' Mrs Sloman enquired with icy politeness. 'Were you addressing us?'

'That's what she said, didn't she?'

'I'm afraid I don't quite – '

'Juliet,' Doreen said with dangerous calm. 'When she saw that Romeo had taken poison.'

'Oh, you're quoting Shakespeare,' Mrs Sloman exclaimed with relief. 'That's charming.'

'It wasn't meant to be,' Doreen muttered darkly.

As the party proceeded in a long crocodile towards the Roman amphitheatre, Ken hung back till he was walking beside Doreen.

'I haven't wanted to open a painful subject with you, Miss Wilkins – '

'You can call me Doreen.'

'Okay, Doreen. But that remark you made to me this morning and your performance just now makes it pretty obvious.'

'Makes what obvious?'

'That you think there was something – well, unexplained about your friend's death.'

'I'm bloody well sure there was!' Doreen burst out with a violence which no one would ever have expected from the quiet girl who had joined the party at Gatwick. 'She wasn't suffering from food poisoning! And it couldn't have been those ice-creams because we both had them. It was terrifying the speed at which she deteriorated. Even the doctors were taken by surprise.'

'What was their opinion – I mean, when she died?'

'It was hard to tell. You see, I don't speak Italian and their English was pretty incomprehensible. But I've seen enough of the inside of hospitals to know when something's not right.'

'So what do you think is the explanation?'

'I can't explain it.' Doreen gave a sigh of despair. 'But I'm convinced that she had a lethal dose of poison in her. And since Alice wouldn't have taken it herself that means it was administered by someone else. But I couldn't get the Italian doctors to take me seriously.'

They had emerged into the main square, named with unconscious humour Piazza Bra. And there, rising in the middle of the entourage of modern buildings, was the incongruous brown mass of the Roman Amphitheatre, built centuries before the Borgias had made a science and an art of poisoning.

'Were either of you carrying drugs that could have been fatal if taken in too large doses?'

'Neither of us had anything like that and anyway we're not such complete idiots – '

'Steady on! I'm just checking out possibilities. Could she have taken something poisonous by accident?'

'It's not something that can easily happen by accident. I mean, poisons as lethal as that are not just lying around.'

Ken grabbed her as she was about to step off the kerb to cross the road, having by habit looked the wrong way.

'Take care, for God's sake! That car only just missed

G

you. So you believe that someone administered poison deliberately. Did you go to the police?'

'No. It was all too complicated. The doctors said there would be an autopsy and that the police would be notified in the normal way. And, you see, it does sound incredible. Why would anyone want to poison Alice, the gentlest and most unselfish of people? But if it was done on purpose it was done by someone on this package tour. That's why I decided to continue the tour.'

'And do a little detective work. You realize that if your theory was correct you could be in a very dangerous position.'

'I know,' Doreen said calmly, obstinately refusing to quicken her pace though a Fiat driver swished past within inches of her. 'That's why I'm telling you. If anything similar happens to me you'll know the reason why.'

Ken halted as they reached the far side of the street. They both had to screw their eyes up against the blazing sun.

'Why choose me? For all you know I might be the person who did it.'

'I know. You're definitely on my list. And you needn't think that all this charm and concern cuts any ice with me at all.'

She gave him a curt nod and stalked off to join the group which was assembling at the entrance to the Arena. Shaking his head ruefully, he strolled after her.

'This Arena—' Gabriella's hand was gesturing towards the double tier of arches curving away behind her—'is the best preserved of all Roman amphitheatres. The interior is an ellipse of 44.50 by 77.58 metres and the tiers of seats can accommodate 22,000 people . . .'

Admirable as was Gabriella's memory for figures and dates Ken could not give his attention to the explanations. As he wandered, always trying not to stray from Diana, across the vast floor of the Arena, his mind kept going back to the figure with the knife which had crept into her room. Even more than Doreen he had grounds for believing that, if a murderer was at work, he must be a member of, or at least have some connection with this tour of the Cities and Lakes. Yet it was impossible to think of any motive which would explain a desire to kill three such harmless women as Mrs Rayburn, Alice Norman and Diana Meredith.

He saw Gabriella glancing at him in puzzlement several times as she led her party through the Piazza delle Erbe, with its huddle of circular umbrellas shading the colourful stalls of the market, and knew that he was being a very bad sightseer. The feeling that he ought to do something nagged at him and yet, what could he do except call in the police? That would certainly bring the tour to an abrupt halt and offer little chance of solving a mystery which had its roots in Padua, Venice and Gatwick.

If he had been in the UK he would have found it easier to decide what to do, but the Italian police were an unknown quantity. What chances were there of getting over to them his growing suspicion that all these things were linked – the thefts, the attacks, Mrs Rayburn's disappearance, Alice Norman's death? Even through an efficient interpreter it would sound pretty lame. About one thing, though, he was able to make up his mind. He'd advise Gabriella to tell Sampson he must come out and join the tour and take the responsibility for decision off her.

The Italian girl was assembling her party, some of whom had wilted and slunk back to the hotel, among the tombs of the ancient family who had once been Lords of Verona. 'This monument commemorates the hospitality which Cangrande della Scala showed to Dante when the poet was exiled from Florence. If you have read the *Divine Comedy* you will remember that Dante speaks of a Greyhound that will come to save Man. Most commentators believe that this was a reference to Cangrande.'

'Does Cangrande mean Greyhound, then?' Gareth Jones asked, his interest tickled by this link with his favourite form of sport.

'Literally it means Big Dog. The Scala were all dogs. Mastino means Mastiff and Cansignorio means Lord Dog.'

'Lord of the Doges,' suggested Mrs Sloman, 'would sound much more appropriate.'

'For a pun like that, Lucy,' observed Mrs Hayward, 'you deserve to be shot.'

The highlight of the evening was to be a performance, at the Roman Theatre, of Shakespeare's *Tempest*. It was being given in English by a visiting company from St Nicholas's College, Cambridge. To Gabriella's disappointment only ten of her party had put their names down to see the play. Mrs Hayward and Mrs Sloman had disagreed bitterly over the interpretation of some passage in the *Divine Comedy* and were not for the moment on speaking terms. Mrs Sloman was for once on her own. Miss Foxell and Mr Tasker were safe bets for anything that smacked of culture. The Prestons were dragging their children along for educational reasons. Diana had persuaded Doreen Wilkins to make up a threesome with herself and Ken, mainly to rescue her from the condolences of the Grants and Joneses or the embarrassingly coy approaches of Mr Benson.

The performance was enthusiastic and only in places spoilt by an impression of amateurism. It was the setting which made up for anything that the performance lacked, with the hill rising behind, the river winding past below and the lights of the city providing a backcloth. Ken found himself strangely affected as the youthful actor, his face virtually invisible behind grey whiskers and beard, declaimed Prospero's familiar speech.

'Our revels now are ended, these our actors,
    As I foretold you, were all spirits, and
    Are melted into air, into thin air:
    And, like the baseless fabric of this vision,

The cloud capped towers, the gorgeous palaces,
The solemn temples, the great globe itself,
Yea, all which it inherit, shall dissolve,
And, like this insubstantial pageant faded,
Leave not a rack behind . . .'

After a couple of hours on the uncompromising stone tiers it was a relief to stand up again.

'I think the Romans must have had very well-padded bottoms,' Diana said feelingly as she straightened.

'Or else they brought cushions as I see most of the locals have done.'

As the three of them emerged on to the road running alongside the Adige Ken suggested: 'What about a walk along the river before going back to the hotel?'

'I think I'll go straight back,' Doreen said. A few hours in the company of Ken and Diana had made her realize that on a moonlit walk by the river she would only be a gooseberry. 'I'm really quite tired. But thanks for taking me in tow.'

Diana put her arm through Ken's as soon as they were clear of the crowd emerging from the theatre.

'You will come tonight, won't you?'

'Yes. That slash on my arm needs a new dressing.'

He did not add that quite apart from his desire to make love again he was not going to let her sleep alone while this vague threat hung over the tour.

'I suppose it's bad tactics for a woman to invite a man to her room so blatantly. Believe me, it's not just because I'm hungry for sex.'

'I wouldn't have thought a woman like you need ever be sex-starved. Most men would –'

'That's just it,' she cut in. 'Most men not only would but unashamedly try to. That's what's so difficult about being a widow or a divorcee. Men seem to assume that you're craving for sex and want nothing better than to leap into bed with them.'

'And you never do?' She had spoken so vehemently that

he put the question hesitantly.

'Which do you mean – crave or leap?'

'Crave.'

'Oh, frequently! You can't have a full sex life for more than ten years and then suddenly become chaste without something screaming. But the attitude of so many men makes it hopeless. They somehow manage to imply that they know you want it and they'll be doing you a terrific favour by supplying your needs. All they're after is a free bang, of course. Most of them have wives of their own. For a widow it's even worse.'

She paused in her tirade and glanced round at him. 'A widower is in a much better position, isn't he? He at least can choose.'

'Yes,' Ken reflected. 'Women were very sweet to me. One or two of my wife's friends were surprisingly ready to fill the gap. But as most of their husbands were pals of mine I didn't really think I could take up the offer.'

'That's a very old-fashioned attitude. From what I hear a lot of husbands don't seem to mind if their wives sleep around. It gives them the chance to do the same.'

'That wasn't the case with me,' Ken said, trying not to sound stiff and pompous. 'It wasn't in the past and it wouldn't be in the future.'

'Yes, darling. But you see you have the capacity to satisfy a woman.'

'How do you mean exactly?' he asked with interest.

She laughed and squeezed his arm tighter. 'Surely you must know. And if you don't I'm certainly not going to give you a lesson in masculine anatomy.'

Ken was silent, slightly puzzled but at the same time pleased and flattered. The sound of an ambulance, forcing its way through the traffic which still thronged the central streets of the city, echoed across the river. The rising and falling wail of its siren gradually increased in volume till they saw its white shape cross the Ponte Garibaldi and head up the Viale Bixio towards the hospital to the north of the town. The reminder that illness and injury can be waiting just round the corner destroyed the mood of confidence that was growing up between them. For the rest of the walk they talked not about themselves but the other members of the party.

As they approached the entrance to their hotel they saw a Fiat 124 saloon and a police car parked outside it. Nearly all the members of the tour were gathered in the hall, talking in little worried groups, or glancing through the glass door of the small sitting-room where the TV set was installed. Two uniformed police officers sat at the table, flanked by Gabriella and Mr Preston at either end. Mrs Hayward was sitting in an upright chair a little apart, her determined little face set and angry. Facing them was a small, fairly young Italian who kept having to wipe the tears from his cheeks.

'What's happened?' Ken asked Tasker, who was standing by himself.

'It's Mrs Sloman. This Italian ran over her. Now of course he's putting on a big act about how upset he is. But it's a bit late now. The way they drive, you wonder it doesn't happen more often.'

'Well, he did at least stop and wait for the police and ambulance to arrive,' Gareth Jones pointed out. 'And he prevented them from moving her till the stretcher-bearers came.'

'Where did it happen?'

'About a quarter of a mile away. The Prestons were quite close and young Nigel ran back to the hotel here to get help. She'd been to the play, hadn't she?'

'Yes. Mrs Meredith and I saw her starting back on her own. I wonder if Miss Wilkins saw anything?'

'I don't think so,' Gareth Jones said. 'She got in before all this happened and went straight up to her room.'

The police officers were getting up, apparently satisfied with the preliminary statements they'd heard. They came out of the room with the dejected Italian between them and bundled him into the back of the police car, where another *vigile* was sitting. One of the officers slid into the Fiat and the two cars drove away.

'I feel rather sorry for the poor devil,' Preston was saying to Mrs Hayward as they came out. 'Frankly I don't think it was his fault.'

'If he hadn't been going so fast,' Mrs Hayward declared, 'he would have been able to stop in time. Lucy would never have tried to cross against the lights.'

'But if he was telling the truth when he said that someone pushed her –'

'Rubbish! They always say that. And he hasn't a single witness to prove it.'

'Witnesses have a peculiar tendency to melt away,' Preston maintained, fingering the golf club tie which he had put on for the Shakespeare play. 'If you've ever had a car accident, you'll know. There were a lot of people waiting for the lights to change. You know how they shove and push.'

'I don't understand why you're on his side.' Mrs Hayward's normally strong voice for once faltered with emotion.

She dabbed at her eyes with a handkerchief and peered round till she found Gabriella.

'Gabriella, could you get a taxi for me, dear? I feel I must go up to the hospital and see that everything possible's being done. Poor Lucy, I can't bear to think of her alone surrounded by foreigners.'

As Gabriella took Mrs Hayward towards the reception desk Ken managed to intercept Preston.

'Did you get a clear picture of what happened?'

'Far from clear, old boy. We were coming back from the play – you were there, weren't you? – we stopped to buy a couple of ice-creams for the children from one of those street dispensers. Mrs Sloman was a little way ahead by the time we moved on, say a hundred yards. We heard this terrific squeal of tyres and then a hell of a lot of shouting. By the time we got there –'

'Did this happen at the traffic lights?'

'Yes.' Preston looked round the little circle which had formed to listen – the Grants, the Joneses, Messrs Benson and Tasker. 'Just down the Via Mazzini. By the time we got there a crowd had formed. At first we didn't realize it was Mrs Sloman. All we could see was this body under the car. The front wheel had passed over her before he could stop. Then I went in to help the driver, who was trying to prevent them dragging her on to the pavement. We saw that her breathing passages were clear and kept her there till the ambulance men came. Just as well, I think she had bad internal injuries.'

'She was breathing?' Benson asked.

'Yes, she was breathing, but she wasn't conscious. She had a shocking contusion on her forehead. I think the front bumper must have hit her.'

'So it looks pretty bad?'

'Yes.' Preston nodded and kept his eyes fixed on the ground. 'It looked bad.'

As the coach moved away from the hotel in Verona next morning the number of unoccupied seats had gone up to four. In addition to those of Mrs Rayburn and Alice Norman there were now Mrs Sloman's and Mrs Hayward's. The latter had decided to stay in Verona, so that she could visit her friend regularly and keep the Italian doctors up to the mark. The latest bulletin had been that Mrs Sloman was still unconscious but there was now more hope of her recovery.

The atmosphere in the coach was subdued and apprehensive. Everyone by now had at least become aware that some kind of a jinx was on this tour. There was no way of telling how many had come to the conclusion that something more than bad luck or coincidence lay behind the thefts, the disappearance, the poisoning, the accident.

Gabriella sat, silent and worried, in her seat at the front of the coach. Mrs Sloman's mishap had prevented the

discussion which she and Ken had arranged; by the time she
got back from the hospital with Mrs Hayward he had gone
up to bed. The way she kept avoiding his eye made him
suspect that she had tried to telephone his room and, on
receiving no answer, had drawn the conclusion that he was
in someone else's.

Whatever she thought, it just could not be helped. Ken
made no bones about sitting beside Diana for the trip round
the shores of Lake Garda, a drive of a hundred miles with
the road hugging the edge of the water. It provided some
of the most spectacular scenery in the whole of Northern
Italy.

The most cheerful person in the coach was Joe. Today's
trip gave him the chance to exercise his professional skill
as a driver, to see that he brought his passengers safe to
their journey's end and gave them a smooth ride. That
meant making clean, well-timed gear changes, delicate foot-
work on the clutch, thinking well ahead to avoid any
necessity for sharp braking, taking the best line on bends
to cut swaying down to a minimum.

At the lake fishing port of Peschiera they had their first
glimpse of the vast stretch of blue water, sparkling under
the morning sun, the mountains behind them blurred by
the heat haze.

'On a day like this it's hard to believe that we weren't
just letting our imaginations run away with us,' Diana said.
The night before in her room Ken had phoned down for
a bottle of his favourite Frascati wine and they had sat on
the balcony for an hour discussing the latest in the series
of casualties. 'It may just be a run of bad luck, Ken. Now
that we've had three casualties that may be the end of it.'

Like Gabriella and most other women, Diana firmly
believed that misfortunes came in threes.

'Let's hope you're right. All the same I still think it
would be a good idea for us to find out what we can about
our fellow passengers. But I want you to promise me one
thing. Never let yourself be left alone with any other single

person and for God's sake don't let them guess what you're
up to.'

When the coach stopped at Garda for half an hour's
shopping they separated, each joining a different group.
Ken saw that Diana had been engaged in conversation by
Benson. He himself managed to break through Miss Foxell's
reserve sufficiently to discover that she worked in the public
library at Bury St Edmunds, liked to read metaphysical
poetry and devoted her spare time to book-binding.

He recounted the conversation to Diana as the coach
cleared the outskirts of Garda and approached the cypress-
clad promontory of San Vigilio.

'Anyway,' he concluded, 'she couldn't possibly be the
person I grappled with in Padua. Not enough flesh on her
arms. What did you make of Benson?'

'He's really very knowledgeable. Apparently he's a writer,
mostly of learned theses on his subject, which is the Alien
Priories. He was very thrilled by my asking him questions,
paid me compliments on my intelligence. But he gives me
a creepy feeling, especially with that long nail on his little
finger. However, that's just me. I'd put him down as
completely harmless.'

After days of looking at architecture it was a pleasant
change to contemplate the more natural beauties of the
scenery. Nature, although the greatest of all artists, does
not make you work so hard to understand and appreciate.
The weather at least was being favourable to the tour.
The long lake lay blue under a cloudless sky. On either side
hills rose to summits high enough to seem mysterious and
unattainable. Every few miles the coach passed through
small lakeside ports where fishing boats lay sheltered in
compact little harbours. From time to time the rugged,
uncompromising cliffs flanking the road gave way to grassy
slopes where olives, fruit trees or an occasional vineyard
flourished.

The second stop was at Malcesine, where the lake had
narrowed like a fjord and the closeness of the hills painted a

deeper shade of blue on the water.

'We have an hour here,' Gabriella announced as the coach drew up near the small station at the base of the cableway. 'So those of you who have a good head for heights may like to take the cableway up to Monte Baldo. There you will be five thousand feet above sea level, so it is wise to take something warm to put on.'

'Not for me, thank you,' Mrs Jones said decisively. 'Since I saw *Where Eagles Dare* I haven't fancied these cable cars much.'

Gareth Jones tilted back the ridiculous little straw hat he had bought at Garda and looked wistfully up at the precipice above.

'What about you, Mother?' Mr Grant asked his wife anxiously. To match his friend he had purchased an equally incongruous peaked cap.

'Terra firma for me,' Mrs Grant decided, after one glance at the two pairs of cables lancing up the mountainside. One of the cars, like a small tram dangling from the sagging wire cable, was just completing the last stages of the descent. 'It makes me giddy just to look at it.'

The party was clearly going to split in two, for Nigel and Emma Preston had said they were determined to make the trip to Monte Baldo. Jim and Jean were obviously of the same mind.

'If you hurry,' Gabriella told them, 'you may just catch the next car. It will be starting as soon as this one gets down.'

'I'm going with them,' Diana told Ken, coming to a sudden decision. 'You stay with the terra firma people.'

'Do you think that's a good idea?' he said doubtfully, but before he could make any objection she had hurried off to tack herself on to Jim and Jean. Climbing last out of the coach, Mr Tasker, his photographic apparatus dangling from his shoulders, set off in pursuit of the seven who were making for the cableway station. He moved with an odd scuttling run, designed to cover the ground fast without shaking up his precious equipment.

Ken, suddenly wishing that he had not agreed to Diana going so far out of sight, had half a mind to follow when Benson's hand on his injured arm made him wince.

'Charming woman, your friend Mrs Meredith. We had a most interesting talk at Garda.'

'Yes, so she told me. I hear you're an expert on the Dissolution of the Monasteries — '

'Not the Dissolution of the Monasteries,' Benson corrected primly. 'The Alien Priories up to the time of Henry the Sixth. Are you interested in history?'

'I don't know much, but I'm very interested in it,' Ken said. He had acquired an instinctive dislike and distrust of Benson, but he would have to overcome that if he was going to get to know him better. At least he had the man under his eye down here on terra firma. If Benson had decided to follow Diana on the cable car Ken would have gone too.

They drifted together towards the lakeside, following the Grants and Joneses who had hurried on as if anxious to be left on their own. It would not be easy, Ken reflected, to break into that little group. But the mere fact of their solidarity was reassuring. If there really was a sinister presence on the tour it was hard to believe that it lurked in any of those four uxorious bosoms.

Benson was discoursing on the Congress of Europe held at Verona in 1822, and the importance of Peschiera in the Italian Wars of Independence. As they reached the lake shore Ken was able to look back towards Monte Baldo. The cable car had begun its fifteen-minute ascent and the bright red cabin had risen far enough to be visible above the roofs of the houses. It seemed much too small to contain a score of passengers as it slowly crept upwards against the face of the mountain.

'Odd chap, that fellow Tasker,' Benson remarked. 'Have you tried to talk to him? He's as close as a clam. I suppose he must have a job back home but I'm blessed if I can find out what he does. Lighthouse keeper, I should imagine.'

'Why do you say that?'

'Seems to prefer his own company to anybody else's. You notice he's always alone? I tried to persuade him to join me last night and he quite snubbed me.'

Benson had offered Ken an unexpected chance to find out what he had been doing when Mrs Sloman had been knocked down by the car. He tried not to show too much eagerness in following it up.

'You weren't at the play, were you?'

'No. For me Shakespeare must be done either very professionally or not at all. I decided to have a look at the night life of Verona. I say, do you feel like a drink? This terrace looks very attractive.'

'Good idea,' Ken agreed. The notion of Benson sampling the night life of Verona was so bizarre that he felt he must probe further.

They secured a table on a terrace that had been built out over the water. It offered magnificent views of the lake in either direction and of the hills flanking it.

Benson ordered a *citron pressé* and Ken a Campari soda.

'I wouldn't have thought Verona had much to offer in the way of night life,' Ken said. 'Apart from the cafés in the Piazza Bra.'

'Oh, you'd be surprised,' said Benson, with an uncharacteristic smirk. The pollen count must have been high, because he had taken his inhaler from his pocket and was applying it to his nose between sentences. 'It's there if you know where to find it. That's the advantage of the Continent over England. Of course, I know it is illegal in Italy now but the Italians have ways of getting round the law and it can be done with discretion and taste. You have to pay a bit over the odds, of course.'

This was very man-to-man stuff, but, coming from Benson, it was peculiarly embarrassing.

'You get good value for your money, though?' he suggested.

'Excellent value. It was all the more of a shock to come

back and find that such a terrible accident had befallen Mrs Sloman.'

So, while Diana and he had been watching the antics of Caliban Mr Benson had been sampling the delights of a *bordello* – or so he would have it believed.

Ken stared up towards Monte Baldo. The cable car was a mere speck of scarlet against the pine trees which clung to the steep upper slopes.

'This tour seems to have been dogged by bad luck, doesn't it – '

'Yes,' Benson agreed, his manner suddenly becoming serious. 'A death and an accident that may result in death. You call that bad luck?'

'What do you call it?'

'Well, I wouldn't call it luck. There must be more than chance in this.'

Benson turned his stare directly on to Ken. The small, circular lenses of his glasses reflected the vivid colours of the lake and hills, so that it was impossible at that instant to see the eyes beyond them.

'But you and Mrs Meredith are of a like opinion, aren't you?'

'Oh?'

'Yes. Otherwise why have you agreed to separate and find out what you can about your fellow travellers?'

'This is supposed to be a very good place for wild flowers. They say it's because Monte Baldo escaped the last Ice Age, so that many plants are to be found here which are extinct elsewhere.'

'Do you think we could find some? It would be exciting to take back a flower which is supposed to be extinct.'

'I'm a photographer, not a botanist, you know.'

'Is photography your profession?'

'No,' Tasker said curtly. 'Photography is not the way I earn my living.'

Diana glanced behind her. She had thought that Jim

and Jean were following them along the path that led to the rocky hill dominating the Valley of the Adige but they were not in sight. Presumably, she thought drily, the keen air and the luxuriant vegetation had exercised an aphrodisiac effect on them and they were rolling in the grass, locked in an amorous clinch. The Prestons had stopped at a café which sold ice-cream and possessed a telescope through which, for ten lire, you could look at the lake and towns far below.

So Diana had broken Ken's rule and allowed herself to be alone with Alan Tasker. However, he seemed to have only one purpose in his mind and that was to find the best position for a photograph of the mountains. Up here the tweed jacket which he had worn every day so far seemed less incongruous.

'If you really want to know,' he said, giving her an embarrassed look, 'I'm an undertaker. I don't publicize it for obvious reasons. When people are on holiday they don't want to be reminded of funerals.'

He turned and pointed to a rocky hilltop a few hundred yards away. Having revealed his dread secret he obviously wanted to change the subject quickly.

'That looks like a good place and you should have a chance of finding some interesting wild flowers. They're growing all over the place.'

To turn and leave him now would be blatantly rude, and in any case he seemed to be in a mood for confidences.

She began : 'Aren't you rather – '

'You were going to say aren't I rather young to be an undertaker, weren't you?'

'Well, as a matter of fact I was.'

'It was my father's business,' Tasker said, cutting away from the path and heading for the little hilltop. 'I was still learning the trade when he got struck by lightning out playing golf one day. I really wasn't ready but I decided to take the business on – mostly for Mother's sake. I made a few mistakes at first, mind you. There's a lot more to being a Funeral Director than meets the eye, you know. We have a very strict professional code.'

'Oh, I'm sure,' Diana murmured. She hoped she had not opened the flood-gates and was about to be regaled with the niceties of embalming. It would harmonize badly with the riot of natural beauty around her. 'So you're quite accustomed to being in the presence of death.'

'It's my job,' he said seriously. 'I see death differently from other people. When you face it every day of your life you come to an acceptance that it's just another part of the natural process. Still, I must confess that when I came on this tour I had hoped to escape from it for a while. Whereas, in fact – '

'Yes.' Diana stooped to pluck another wild flower, which she added to her bunch. 'We've had one death and there may well be a second, if Mrs Sloman – '

'It's no business of mine,' Tasker cut in with sudden sharpness. 'There's nothing I can do for these people and I'm in no way involved. That is why I dismiss it from my mind and concentrate on my photography.'

Feeling slightly snubbed, she did not say any more till they reached the top of the hill.

'Ah!' Tasker said. 'This is what I hoped for.'

The far side of the hill, which had been invisible as they approached, dropped sheer away in a precipice of several hundred feet. The sudden discovery of a void beyond the immediate horizon gave Diana a shock. As her gaze dropped to the lake several thousand feet below she instinctively edged back a few steps from the edge of the cliff. Once accustomed to the sensation of height she was able to let her eyes travel with wonder round the vast panorama of mountains. The town of Malcesine was almost directly below. The cars on the road crawled like ants and the craft out on the lake seemed like specks of white dust.

Behind her Alan Tasker was setting up his tripod on a level piece of ground. He squinted through his light meter and carefully adjusted the settings on his camera. She waited

H

while he took half a dozen pictures facing in different directions. Then, just as he was about to remove the camera from the tripod, an idea seemed to strike him. He gave her a quizzical look.

'You know what I would really like? To take one of you against that background. Do you think you could stand on that rock and be looking out over the lake? It would make a fabulous picture. And I promise I'll let you have a copy.'

He had pointed to a rock close to the edge of the cliff. She thought that if she did not look straight down it need not worry her. This particular shot seemed to mean a lot to him.

'All right.' She moved over to the rock he had indicated.

'Could you be facing slightly away, looking down the lake?'

'Like this?'

She turned her head, so that now she could only see him out of the corner of her eye. And suddenly a premonition of danger swept over her. Ken had warned her not to let herself be caught alone with anyone and here she was standing on the edge of a precipice with a man crouched five paces away.

An undertaker whose father had been struck by lightning whilst playing golf!

'Keep quite still,' he commanded.

She felt she had to turn, to see what he was doing.

She surprised the strangest expression on his face, a sort of unholy triumph. She knew that he'd only have to take five quick paces, give her one push and she would have been gone forever.

He straightened up and began to move towards her. Panicked into sudden action she ducked sideways, slipped past him and ran down the hill. Her heart was beating furiously when she regained the path and her bunch of wild flowers was gone. She did not look round. Half walking, half running, she hurried along the path that led back to the little group of buildings where Jim and Jean and the

Prestons were collecting to catch the next cable car down.

'Have you seen Mr Tasker?' Mrs Preston asked, her eyes noting Diana's flushed face and quick breathing. 'He's going to miss it, if he doesn't hurry.'

'He'll be along in a minute, I think. It's a marvellous spot for photographs up here, isn't it?'

Nigel and Emma were studying her with the mercilessly observant eyes of the young. Diana seriously thought that she must look not unlike the victim of an attempted rape. When Alan Tasker joined them, just in time to catch the cable car, she decided to take the bull by the horns and went straight up to him.

'I'm sorry I spoilt your picture, Mr Tasker. It's just that I have a very bad head for heights and I felt a fit of vertigo coming on.'

'I frightened you, didn't I?' He was distressed and sorrowful, his eyes dropping away again whenever he tried to look at her face. 'I was only going to take another reading with my light meter.'

The coach was already waiting for them at the station where the cableway ended its journey, and the other half of the party had already taken their seats. Diana saw at once that Doreen Wilkins was sitting in her place, talking to Ken. She made as if to rise but Diana motioned her to stay where she was. The seat next to Miss Foxell was empty and she sat down in that.

The tour round the lake continued. The party stopped for lunch at the Roxy-Park, Limone di Garda, and ate their meal on the *terrazza*, once again overlooking the lake. Yet somehow the beauty of the setting failed to restore the good spirits of the party, and try as she might Gabriella could not disperse the atmosphere of wariness and gloom which pervaded the coach for the rest of that day's trip. Even Messrs Jones and Grant had discarded their funny hats.

Her party had begun to split up into secretive little cliques and they were never more ill at ease than when in the enforced proximity of the coach. She could sense the mood of relief as Joe threaded his way through the Milan traffic and deposited his passengers outside the Hotel Savoia.

'Proper miserable lot you've got on your hands this time,' Joe commented when the last of the party had dismounted.

'There's a jinx on this tour,' Gabriella said, 'and they can all feel it. Everyone's waiting and wondering what the next thing's going to be.'

'That's the wrong way to look at it,' Joe told her cheerfully. 'If you're looking for troubles they'll come to you, sure as sure. Ten o'clock tomorrow morning?'

'That's right. You're fixed up all right, Joe?'

Joe gave her a wink.

'I'm hoping so. A nice little lay-by, with a hard standing for the coach and a soft bed for me.'

He thought she looked wistful as she smiled back at him before climbing out and hurrying after her charges. Joe engaged a gear and operated his left traffic indicator. He wondered what Pina had dreamed up for him this time. She could always be expected to pull something unexpected out of the hat, that one.

Ken had taken a shower and was just finishing drying himself when he heard a tap on his door. Thinking it might be Diana he quickly put on a shirt and stepped into a pair of slacks before going to open the door.

'Can I come in?' enquired Gabriella, taking obvious pleasure from his surprise.

'Er – yes, of course.'

He held the door open while she walked quickly in and when he closed it, slipped the catch which would prevent it being opened from the outside.

Gabriella glanced down once at his bare feet. Her eyes flickered over his tousled hair, which he had not had time to comb. She was still wearing her blue uniform skirt but she had taken off the cheeky little tambourine hat and discarded her jacket.

'Sorry about the mess,' he said. 'I've just been having a shower.'

'You don't mind my coming like this? I just had to talk to someone.'

'Not a bit. Would you like to sit down? There's only one chair, I'm afraid.'

'It's all right. The bed will do for me.'

She settled herself at the end of the bed, leaning against the headboard with her long, slender legs tucked up under her.

'I've never had a chance to thank you.'

'What for?'

'For being so sweet to me at Padua. You've no idea what a difference it made.'

Ken stooped to take a cigarette from the packet lying on the table. What would Gabriella's reaction be if she knew that the kiss in the hotel manager's office had started a chain reaction which had ended in Diana's bed?

He said: 'Things have not improved much since then, have they?'

'Except the weather. I must say we've been very lucky about that. But you really mean Mrs Sloman's accident, don't you? I told you misfortunes always come in threes, didn't I?'

'If you're right, then we've had our share of accidents for the tour.'

'Do you really think so?' She shook her head as he offered the packet of cigarettes to her. 'What worries me is Miss Wilkins. She's got a funny sort of accusing manner, as if she thought that somebody in the party was responsible for her friend's death.'

'Did she tell you that?'

'Not in so many words, but it's obvious that she's suspicious of everybody. A thing like that is somehow infectious, and I seem to have caught it too. Ken, do you think it's possible – that Mrs Rayburn's disappearance and Miss Norman's death and Mrs Sloman's accident are all linked?'

Ken had found his lighter in the pocket of the jacket he had flung over the chair. He lit his cigarette before answering.

'I must admit that I think it's very possible. That's why I was going to suggest to you that you tell your Mr Sampson he's got to come out and take some of the responsibility off you. It's too much to ask a girl to handle.'

'I don't like to do that. There's only two more days to go. After Milan we've only one more night stop. I don't want him to think I'm not capable of coping.'

'I'm sure you're perfectly capable,' Ken reassured her. 'In fact I think it's amazing the way you've kept your cool. But it does help if you've got someone you can talk things over with and who'll take a share of the responsibility.'

'I know,' Gabriella said, her very large eyes swiftly melting into softness. 'That's why I came to you.'

After a moment's pause he said : 'Doreen Wilkins made it clear she doesn't trust me any more than anyone else in this party. Why should you?'

'Perhaps I'm a better judge of men.'

She uncoiled her legs and swung them over the side of the bed.

'Why are you afraid to come near me?'

'I'm not.'

'Then put down that cigarette and come over here.'

He ignored the command to put down his cigarette but he did walk over and stand close in front of her. She looked up at him, her face on a level with his belt buckle, her lips moist and parted. He had not had time to button up the front of his shirt. Her hands moved up, pushing the material aside, and began to caress his chest, sliding upwards till they found the most sensitively responsive parts. His heart beat faster, pumping blood to the action areas.

She kept her eyes fixed on his face, as if it were a dial

giving her the readings of a turbine that was starting up. The provocation of her finger-tips was becoming intoxicating. He put his hands round the back of her head and pressed her face against him, but she stood up, roughly pushing him away.

At first he thought that this was to be the end of it, that she had been arousing him just to have the pleasure of rejecting him. But Gabriella was already unbuttoning her blue uniform shirt. She peeled it off, unfastened the zip at the side of her skirt and let it slip to the ground. A quick stoop to remove a pair of scarlet panties and she stood proudly naked before him. The stripping operation had taken about ten seconds flat.

She lay down on the bed, her sable hair framing the dark oval face and held her arms out in a gesture of irresistible invitation.

'*Dammi l'amore. Caro, carissimo.*'

This time he did put his cigarette down. He had thought up a convincing lie to explain the bandage on his arm.

CHAPTER VI

'A PENNY for them, Ken.'

It was the first time Ken and Diana had had a chance to be alone since the day's trip had begun. After dinner they had come out to stroll round the streets in the neighbourhood of the Duomo. In order to escape the relentless noise of the Milan traffic they had turned into the covered Galleria Vittorio Emmanuele.

Ken would not have sold his thoughts to Diana for a million lire. He was recalling the energetic half-hour he had spent making love to Gabriella and wondering how it was that he felt no regrets nor any cooling of his feelings towards Diana. Paradoxically these two women, so different in age, shape and temperament, seemed to complement each other. A session with one only made him more eager to make love to the other. But of course there was absolutely no hope of explaining that to a woman.

He said: 'I was just thinking about all the people I talked to today. I'm afraid I'm not much further on, but if I had to put my money on someone I know who it would be.'

'So do I,' Diana said at once. 'That man Tasker.'

'Good God!' Ken said in genuine surprise. 'Do you have any particular reason?'

'I certainly have!'

While they strolled under the arched roof between the shops and cafés which fronted on to the Galleria she told him about the incident at the edge of the cliff on Monte Baldo.

'But perhaps he really did want to have a picture of you,' Ken suggested. 'You're probably very photogenic.'

'You didn't see that extraordinary look on his face.' He felt her shiver and she recalled the terrible moment when she had suddenly become convinced that she had, metaphorically speaking, laid her head on the block.

The look, Ken thought to himself, might have been due to naked lust. Tasker was an odd character, who might easily get his thrills by photographing desirable women against a dramatic background – a sort of photographic rape, which could be repeated in imagination when the picture was printed.

'And I'm sure he's not what he makes himself out to be,' Diana was going on. 'Can you believe that his undertaker father was struck by lightning while playing golf?'

'It has been known to happen,' Ken pointed out mildly. 'And I don't see why an undertaker should be immune.'

They had come to the end of the Galleria. A shower of rain was beginning to fall and people were crowding in for shelter from the streets outside. At the nearby café, whose tables spilled out on to the marbled footway, the orchestra embarked on a soulful interpretation of '*Torni a Sorrento*'.

Diana and Ken turned round and began to retrace their steps.

'You obviously don't think much of my theory,' she said. 'Who's this person you'd put your money on?'

'Benson. He went out of his way to let me know that when Mrs Sloman was pushed under the car he was enjoying himself in a Veronese brothel.'

'Mr Benson in a brothel?' Diana repeated, one eyebrow raised disbelievingly. 'That's even more hard to swallow than the thunderstruck undertaker. And in any case you've forgotten one thing. You said you thought the person who broke into my room was a woman.'

'I said I thought it might be. But I'm inclined to think that you were right when you said that episode was part of the pattern of thefts and nothing to do with the deaths. Otherwise nothing makes any sense at all.'

'Unless there are two people working together. A married couple, for instance.'

Ken was steering Diana towards a gay Espresso bar he had noticed farther back down the Galleria. He stopped to look at her thoughtfully.

'The Grants or the Joneses?'

'Or Jim and Jean,' Diana said quietly.

Ken shook his head. 'It passes the bounds of credibility. Tasker, I'll grant you, is a possibility but those three couples – no, I can't believe it. How about a coffee while I tell you why my money goes on Benson?'

It was close to midnight when they got back to the hotel. They had made friends with a Milanese who was glad of the chance to practise his English and insisted on showing them the comparatively quiet thirteenth-century square with the well in the middle which had supplied water when the city was the capital of the Roman Empire.

Ken minded less about being seen in the company of Diana by his fellow tourists than by Gabriella, but, as they collected their keys from the night reception clerk, the hotel foyer was deserted.

'Your room or mine?' Diana whispered as they walked towards the lift.

'Yours.' Ken made the decision without hesitation. He was afraid that his own room might bear traces of Gabriella's visitation.

'I'm number 203, but I think all our rooms are on the same floor. I know Mr Benson is in number 216, which is just opposite mine.'

The automatic doors of the lift jerked back with a clatter which must have been very disturbing for the occupants of nearby rooms. Even to close them again, Ken had to exert force and bang them hard.

With a guilty sense that they must be disturbing the whole corridor they tiptoed to Diana's door.

'You open it.' She handed Ken the key. 'I don't know why but I don't want Mr Benson to hear us.'

Ken inserted the key, which, despite his care, turned with a loud click. Making a rueful expression he held the door to let her pass. He was about to close it when she stopped.

'I heard something,' she whispered.

'What?'

'Listen. It was like a sort of groaning.'

He stood, cocking his ears, then moved out into the passage again. A shuffling, bumping sound was coming from beyond the door of number 216, accompanied by muffled and confused grunts.

'That's Benson's room, isn't it?'

'Yes. At least I saw him go into it. Do you think we ought to – ?'

Ken had moved across the corridor and put his ear against the panel of the door. He had no difficulty in pin-pointing the sounds as coming from inside the room.

'I'm not too sure about this. I think you ought to go into your room and leave it to me.'

'I'm going to wait and see what happens,' Diana said obstinately. 'What are you going to do?'

Ken did not answer. He bunched his fist and rapped sharply on the door.

'Benson! Are you all right?'

The reaction was a series of heavy bumps, like someone banging their feet on the floor. The muffled grunts became louder but were quite indistinguishable as words.

'I'm going to break this door down,' Ken said decisively. 'I want you to stay in your own room.'

'Try the handle,' Diana suggested. 'It may not be locked.'

To Ken's surprise, when he tried the handle he found that she was right. The door swung open in response to his push. Inside, the room was dark. The noises had stopped. He reached in, felt for the light switch and turned it on.

The room was in a state of wild disorder. Drawers had been ransacked, shirts and underwear lay scattered over the floor, a couple of suitcases had been opened and their contents tipped out on the carpet.

At first number 216 seemed deserted. It was only when he walked right in that he saw Benson, lying on the floor at the foot of the bed.

He had been trussed in a crude but effective way with two lengths of blue nylon rope. One was lashed round his ankles. The other, securing his wrists in the small of his back, was finished off by a slip-knot at the front of his body where his hands could not reach it. A face towel from the bathroom had been torn in two, knotted in the middle and then tied at the back of his neck to form a rough gag.

There was an ugly bruise on his forehead. The blow had been hard enough to break the skin and one side of his face was covered with congealing blood.

'Diana!' Ken called. 'Come and give me a hand.'

He was kneeling beside Benson, working on the tight knot at the back of his neck, as she came in. She stopped short, shocked by the sight of the bloody face and the atmosphere of violence and chaos all around.

'See if you can find a knife or something,' Ken told her. 'These knots look a bit too tight for fingers.'

By the time Diana came back from her room with a pair of scissors, Ken had managed to unfasten the strip of towel and free Benson's mouth from the bunched knot that blocked it. He drew in a wheezing breath and spat out several fragments of wet white stuff.

'Please undo my hands. They're going dead.'

'I'm going to have to roll you on your side to get at this knot.'

'All right, but please hurry.'

'For God's sake,' Ken said, as he saw the nail-scissors Diana had brought. 'Is that the best you can do?'

The slip-knot had been pulled tight with a strong jerk and the ends left dangling. It took Ken half a minute of hacking with the tiny scissors to cut through the nylon. He had to help Benson free his lacerated wrists before he sat him up with his back against the bottom of the bed.

Benson looked ghastly with the half-dried blood on his face glinting under the overhead light. He straightened his arms painfully, moving the fingers to get the circulation going again.

'Can you see my glasses anywhere? Everything's a blur.'

'Just a sec. Let me get your ankles free, and then we'll have a look at that head of yours.'

'Here are your glasses.' Diana stooped and picked the pair of gold-rimmed spectacles from the rug at the side of the bed. 'But I think I'd better clean your face up before you try to put them on.'

Benson did not attempt to rise. He just sat there on the floor, leaning his back against the bed, while Diana knelt beside him and gently sponged the blood away from his brow and cheek. The cut, once clean, was not so bad as it had looked, but the discoloration of a nasty bruise was already apparent.

'What happened?' Ken put the question as soon as he felt that Benson had been made comfortable enough to talk.

Benson put his glasses on with shaking hands, his eyes screwed up under the glare of the hanging bulb.

'Do you think you could turn that light off? My head's bursting.'

'Yes, of course,' Diana said, moving quickly to the wall. She switched on the low shaded bedside lamp and extinguished the overhead light.

'Ah, that's better.' Benson was still massaging his wrists and wriggling his toes. He was a pathetic and almost comic sight in his rumpled tropical suit. 'I'm afraid I've very little idea what happened. All I know is that when I came into my room this evening, something hit me before I could even turn on the light and when I came to I was on the floor where you found me.'

He blinked round at the chaotic mess in the room.

'Oh my goodness! What on earth – '

'It was obviously a thief,' Ken said. 'Have you anything valuable he might have been after?'

Benson instinctively put his hand inside his jacket.

'My wallet. It's gone.'

'There's a wallet over here,' Diana said, stooping to pick a leather object from a pile of socks and handkerchiefs.

'Can I see, please?'

Benson flipped the wallet open, searched through the compartments.

'That's odd. All my Italian currency is here as well as a traveller's cheque for fifty pounds and my Access card.'

'Funny sort of thief. How long ago did this happen?'

Benson peered at his watch. 'It seems ages. I thought no one would ever hear me. In fact, I suppose I've been here about two hours. It must have been about ten when I came up to my room.'

'Two hours gives him a pretty good start.' Ken straightened up and moved towards the telephone. 'Still, we must inform the police and then see about getting a doctor for you.'

'I don't think it will be much good,' Benson said with resignation. 'I can't give any description, and as for calling a doctor I don't think he can do any more than you two have done. I can't tell you how grateful I am.'

'I'm going to call the hotel manager.' Ken had already picked up the phone. 'For all we know there may have been other attacks tonight.'

'Well, that rules out Benson. I feel rather a swine now for having all those suspicions about him.'

'Yes. He was really a very pathetic sight. I thought the doctor was remarkably casual about the whole thing. When you pay twenty quid you expect something more than advice to have a good night's sleep and take things easy.'

'The detective wasn't much better. He seemed to regard it as perfectly normal that a foreign tourist should be hit over the head and his room ransacked. The whole thing just seemed a bore to him. Perhaps he'd have shown some real interest if Benson had been killed.'

'I've heard that the crime rate in Milan is terribly high. I must say I'm very thankful I don't have to sleep alone after what's happened.'

It was well after half past two in the morning. Ken and

Diana were sitting in the latter's room, letting their nerves calm down over a bottle of the now familiar Frascati wine.

'That's the fourth time the belongings of someone on this tour have been ransacked,' Ken said thoughtfully. 'There's something more here than just coincidence or even common theft. It's more like a search and it is being carried out by some member of our party.'

'That makes eight separate incidents in the space of five days,' Diana pointed out. 'At Gatwick Mrs Rayburn missed the plane and subsequently vanished. In Venice my room was searched and Alice Norman got stomach poisoning. In Padua the Joneses' luggage was rifled, the Prestons' room turned upside down, and then there was that terrifying business of the person with the knife. In Verona Mrs Sloman gets run over in the street and receives injuries which may still prove fatal, and here in Milan Mr Benson is knocked unconscious and robbed. Don't you think this tour ought to be stopped, right here and now?'

'If the tour is stopped there will be no hope of ever finding out what lies behind it all and a thief and a murderer may go scot free. As Gabriella points out, we have only one more night together, because we fly back on the same evening as we do the sights of Turin. Myself, I'd be in favour of seeing it through, especially as our list of candidates is gradually being reduced.'

'The police may decide otherwise – or the tour operators.' Diana slipped her shoes off and went to sit on the little stool in front of her dressing-table.

'Each of these incidents has been dealt with by a different municipal police force, you must remember. It is only we who are on the tour who can see a sinister connection between them. And if the tour was abandoned now what could they do with us? And how much damage would be done to the reputation of Connoisseur Tours?'

She put her hands up to unfasten her necklace, laid it on the dressing-table and swung round to face him. 'Yes. I see. But will you promise me one thing? That from now

on you'll stay very close to me and never let it happen that
I'm left alone with Mr Tasker?'

The murmur of traffic from beyond the double-glazed
window had gradually slackened until now there was only
the swish of an occasional vehicle passing. They drank their
last glass of wine without speaking but knowing that the
mood and atmosphere was changing.

Then Diana stood up and presented the back of her full-
length dress to him.

'Will you undo my zip for me? I won't pretend I can't
reach it but it feels much more delicious when you do it.'

A little later, as she lay in his arms, she suddenly raised
her head from the pillow.

'Darling, you don't use perfume, do you?'

He was instantly alert. She must have picked up the
scent of the perfume which Gabriella used. A moment of
crisis had come just when he least expected it. He
contemplated an easy lie and then rejected it.

'No,' he said. 'I don't.'

'There's a very subtle perfume in your hair. Diorella,
I think. Is it Gabriella's?'

Ken's heart was beating faster, this time with apprehen-
sion. 'Yes. It's Gabriella's.'

Diana snuggled closer to him. 'Thank you, darling.
I knew it was but I'm glad you told me.'

Ken pondered for a long moment.

'You don't mind?'

'I claim no ownership over you, darling. And I can't
complain that it has taken the edge off your appetite. Quite
the contrary, in fact.'

Ken was glad that he had turned the light out. His face
might have shown his astonishment. He was beginning to
realize that even at his time of life he still had a lot to
learn about women.

There was little danger during the next day of Diana finding
herself alone with Alan Tasker. As the party, ferried by Joe

from place to place, visited in succession the Duomo, the Brera Art Gallery and the Biblioteca Ambrosiana, all its members kept close together, with the self-protective instinct of a herd of roebuck when a lion is on the prowl. All were making a brave attempt to pretend they were enjoying themselves, getting the very most out of their package tour, but the sight of Benson, with a spectacular bandage round his head, was a constant reminder. It would have been a very obtuse person who had not worked out by now that an unnamed threat lay over them all. Benson, paradoxically, seemed to be in better form than anyone and quite recovered from his mishap. Since breakfast, when the facts had come out, he had assumed the role of hero of the party. His gratitude to Ken and Diana was almost embarrassing, especially as he showed it by constantly tagging on to them. It was hard to shake him off without being unashamedly rude.

Doreen Wilkins remained darkly mysterious and observant but she was beginning to flag a little in her attempts to probe her companions' secrets. The Prestons, who had obviously had a family conference, kept close together and made no attempt to fraternize with the other groups. Apart from them, the most closely-knit little clique was the Grants and Joneses, who now said very little except when they were out of earshot of the rest. Miss Foxell remained faithful to her guide-book and the little loose-leaf note-book in which she constantly made jottings, whilst Alan Tasker continually took photographs with one or other of his two cameras. Jim and Jean, who had never once changed out of their sets of blue jeans, clung even more closely together than before, although Jean was taking less and less notice of the paintings and architectural marvels which Gabriella pointed out.

In Gabriella herself Ken noticed a subtle change. The performance was still flawless, the explanations and introductory patter in the coach as polished as ever. But her mind seemed to be elsewhere and she gave the impression

I

of an actress speaking her lines automatically at a matinee. Only once did the large eyes rest on Ken and he fancied he saw a sad reproach in them. Gabriella had been present when the detective had listened to Diana's and Ken's statement that they had heard Benson's struggles at the moment when they were about to enter her room.

The last visit, before the coach left Milan for Como, was to the Church of Santa Maria delle Grazie, or rather to the Dominican Monastery adjoining it. There, in the empty refectory, sixteen worried and slightly apprehensive tourists stood before Leonardo da Vinci's great masterpiece, gazing up at the thirteen participants in the Last Supper.

And it was in this improbable situation that Ken, for no logical reason, ran his fingers over the material of his trousers just below the waistbelt and felt the key which Diana had confided to him in Venice.

Como was a mere thirty miles to the north of Milan by an *autostrada* which bore the evocative sign '*Ai Laghi*' – 'To the Lakes'. The tour organizers had shown good sense in providing a second day of scenic sightseeing to make a break in the visits to churches, galleries and museums. The following day's itinerary would give the passengers a glimpse of no less than five lakes – Como, Lugano, Varese, Maggiore and Orta. It was the part of the tour which Joe liked best because the steep ascents and descents, the winding roads with their sudden glimpses of sensational views, made the greatest demands on his professional skill as well as on the engine, transmission and suspension of the coach. The run up to Como was just a piece of cake which he polished off in half an hour from door to door.

The Hotel Belvedere was one of the best placed on the whole tour. It stood on the Viale Lungo Lario, facing up the western fjord of the two-pronged lake.

Following her customary practice, Gabriella stood with the reception clerk allocating her passengers to their

respective rooms and seeing that their luggage went to the
right place.

'Mr Jones, I'm putting you and your wife in the room
next to Mr and Mrs Grant. That's what you want, isn't it?
It means we have to put you on the top floor, but the views
are even better there.'

A flashing smile as the key was passed across the counter
made Mr Jones feel that he was the only member of the
party she minded about. He readjusted his new straw hat
to a more cheeky angle and gave her a wink.

'Mr Collins, you and Mrs Collins are in number 328.
It's over in the annexe, but you don't have to leave the
hotel and the room is very quiet. Miss Foxell, you are in
number 68, which looks out over the garden as you
requested, and Mrs Meredith is in number 83.'

As Diana took her key and moved off to claim her suitcase Gabriella glanced up at Ken, who was next in the line.

'Oh, Mr Forsythe, there's a slight query about your room.
Could you possibly wait till I have the others settled?'

Ken kicked his heels in the hallway while Benson, the
Preston family and Tasker were assigned to their rooms.

'What's the query?' he asked, as Gabriella came out from
behind the counter.

'There's no query.' She handed him the key she was
holding. 'You're in number 281, on the top floor. That was
just an excuse because there's something I want to show
you.'

'Oh. What?'

She shook her head and nodded in the direction of the
doorway, where Joe and the head porter were sorting out
the suitcases.

'I don't want to talk about it here. Could you come to
my room in about ten minutes? It's 207, on the same floor
as yours.'

To judge from her elusive expression she had some sort
of mischief up her sleeve.

'All right,' he said, in spite of his better judgement. 'In ten minutes.'

Ken knew from experience that a woman's ten minutes means at least a quarter of an hour. It was twenty minutes later, when he had changed into fresh clothes, that he knocked on the door of number 207.

'*Avanti!*'

The voice only reached him faintly. He opened the door and went in. The sound of running water came from the bathroom.

'I won't be a moment,' Gabriella's voice called.

He slipped the catch on the door and walked over to the window, which she had flung open. The view up the lake was stupendous. The sun had set and the lights along the lake front had already been switched on. But there was still a golden glow in the sky and deep purple pools of shadow lay on the flanks of the hills. The air had become absolutely still and the surface of the water was silkily calm, except for the bow waves of the ferry boats plying to and from the wharf nearer the centre of the town.

'I just had to get out of that uniform. It was so hot and sticky in Milan today, didn't you find?'

She had shaken out her hair, stripped off all her day clothes and put on a kimono-style coat of bottle-green stretch satin which revealed her shape not so much because it was transparent but because it clung and rippled on her body as she moved.

'You don't mind if I do my hair?' she asked, apparently unaware of the impact her appearance had had on him.

'No. Go ahead.'

She stood with her back to him and he wondered whether it was done deliberately so that he could watch the material pulled tight against her curves as she raised her hands to brush her hair.

'As you may have guessed,' she said over her shoulder, 'Sammie decided that the tour should go on. He said that unless the Italian police recommended it, there would be

no advantage in changing our plans. Everybody would have
been stuck in Milan until we could arrange air passages
home.'

'Has anyone else suggested packing up and going home?'

She turned to face him, continuing to comb her hair with
a backward sweeping movement which raised her breasts
at each stroke.

'The Grants and Joneses asked me what we intended to
do, but I think it was only because they were afraid they
would not get their money's worth.'

'I think you've made the right decision. Especially as it's
de-escalating.'

Her brow furrowed as for once she found herself baffled
by an English word.

'I mean that Alice Norman's illness could have been food
poisoning. Mrs Sloman's injuries have not so far proved
fatal, and the attack on Mr Benson was comparatively
restrained.'

'You mean that the violence is lessening – like going down
step by step?'

'Exactly. Now, what was this thing you wanted to show
me?'

She put the brush down on the dressing-table and walked
across to the chest of drawers. Her way of walking, acquired
instinctively as part of her Italian upbringing, was to Ken
more sexually exciting than the shakings of a belly-dancer.
Especially now, when perspiration, or the dampness left by
a shower-bath, combined with the clinging material to
emphasize the movement of every muscle.

When she stooped to open the lowest drawer and take
out a hair band he knew that she was going through a
gamut of the most provocative movements she could devise
with the clear intention of arousing his desire.

She had certainly been successful. He wondered how it
was that for so long he had been unable to find any woman
that satisfied him and now, suddenly, he had the choice.
Not a choice really, for in view of Diana's unexpected

reaction last night, there was no reason why he should not have them both. If Fate deals you a double hand of straight flushes why not play them?

'Joe found this in the coach when he was cleaning it out this morning. It had been pushed down the side of one of the seats.'

He took the key which she handed to him, making an effort to concentrate on something else besides her body. Now that she was close he could smell the Diorella she had sprayed on to herself.

'Do you know where it comes from?'

'It's almost certainly the pass key from the hotel in Padua. The one the thief must have used to get into the Prestons' room.'

And into Diana's, Ken thought. He said: 'Joe found it pushed down beside one of the seats? Do you know which one? You might remember who had been sitting there.'

'I know which seat.' She took the key from him and went to lay it on the top of the chest of drawers. 'But since Padua all sorts of people have sat there – the Preston kids, Jean Collins, Mr Benson, Miss Foxell – '

'Tasker?' Ken moved away from the window and perched on the arm of the one easy chair in the room.

'Mr Tasker? Yes, I think so. It's hard to remember. Do you think I should report it to the police?'

The whole conversation was a pretence. They were both talking as if they had learnt their lines from a script. Gabriella's eyes had that misty, soft look which was a sure sign that she was feeling sexy. He could tell by the quick veiled glances she gave him that she was measuring his response to her ragingly sensuous performance.

'The police where? Here in Como they won't be very interested. I think all you can do is try and get it back to the manager in Padua before he has all the locks changed.'

'That's what I'm going to do. But don't you see that this makes it virtually certain that we have a thief in the party?'

'I know. That's why I'm glad you're continuing the tour. Because when we get back to Gatwick I think we'll know what this has all been about.'

'How will we know?'

'I could be entirely wrong. I'd rather not say any more at the moment.'

Gabriella at last came close to him, began to undo the buttons of his shirt.

'You can tell *me*, though, can't you?'

'No, Gabriella. I'm not going to say any more and you can't get it out of me by seduction.'

She pulled his shirt over his shoulders and down his arms, bent her head to his naked chest and gently bit his nipples. He felt the fire of mounting desire course through him. She pulled the kimono back over her own shoulders. It slid to the floor making a silken pool round her feet.

'Tell me what we'll know when we get back to Gatwick,' she murmured into his ear, following the words up with a flick of her tongue.

'No, my sweet. I said I wouldn't and I'm not going to.'

Suddenly she pushed back from him, her eyes blazing.

'You'll tell *her*, though, won't you?'

He was rocking under the shock of her abrupt change of mood when she put her hands up and raked her nails down the front of his chest.

'There! How are you going to explain that to her?'

He looked down, saw the six parallel weals which her sharp nails had inflicted and knew that he would carry the marks for weeks.

'You little – '

Really angry, he took hold of her, forced her face downwards on to the bed and gave her four hard smacks with the flat of his hand. They echoed like pistol shots and left the reddening imprint of a hand on her bottom.

'That hurt!' Gabriella gasped, putting a hand down to rub her behind.

'Good. It was meant to,' Ken said, reaching for his shirt.

'*Sei una bestia!*' she shouted. '*Non ti voglio piu bene! Mascalzone!*'

She grabbed up the kimono and curled up on the bed, sobbing and hiding her face in the material. Ken did up the buttons of his shirt, made for the door and let himself out.

After dinner, when for the first time Gabriella was not there to see that everything proceeded smoothly, Ken and Diana went out to walk along the esplanade bordering the lake shore. The sky was completely dark now and from out on the water the lights of boats cast shimmering reflections.

'You're very quiet,' Diana said, when they had gone a couple of hundred yards without saying a word. 'Something's happened, hasn't it?'

Ken was still smarting, quite literally, from his encounter with Gabriella. He could feel the marks on his chest tingling and was wondering how on earth he could prevent Diana seeing them, or explain them if she did. Gabriella's revenge had been vindictive and effective. He was smarting mentally too, as he remembered the false confidence she had built up in him with that display of erotic sensuality.

To switch the direction of his thoughts he said: 'I think I've hit on a possible reason for some of these extraordinary things that have been happening. You remember that key you gave me in Venice?'

Diana veered to avoid one of the brash young men who were strolling along the esplanade, looking for girls. He would have bumped into her if she had not moved quickly. He muttered some Italian phrase as he passed, whether an insult or a compliment it was hard to tell.

'The key Mrs Rayburn gave me?'

'Yes. I've been looking at it. You know what I think it is? It's a key to one of those left-luggage lockers where you can deposit your things and take the key away with you.'

'She said that she had found it.' Diana was casting her

mind back, trying to revisualize the episode at Gatwick.
'She wanted to get it to the Lost Property Office before we
took off.'

'Did she tell you where she had found it?'

'She was rather vague about that. I seem to remember
she muttered something about finding it in her bag. She had
a sort of bucket-shaped holdall in which she kept the things
she wanted on the journey. But I don't see how a lost key
could have found its way into her bag.'

The crowd was thickening as they came nearer to the
busy Piazza Cavour. On the other side of the road people
were sitting out on the pavement cafés enjoying the warm
night air. A ceaseless stream of cars moved in both directions
along the Lungo Lario. The ferry-boat from Argegno was
just arriving at the quay and a small crowd of passengers
was already collecting for the return trip up the lake.

'Nor do I. But if its owner realized that's what had
happened he may have wanted it back badly enough to be
prepared to kill her to get it.'

'And if you're right,' Diana said slowly, as if she was
reluctant to face the thought, 'that person is on this tour,
still searching for the key. That explains the breaking into
rooms, Ken, and the ransacking of people's possessions.
But what reason could there be for wanting to kill Alice
Norman and Mrs Sloman? So far as we know their rooms
were not even searched.'

'After they had been taken to hospital it would have been
comparatively simple to search their rooms. The thief would
have had more time and could have carried it out in a
more orderly fashion.'

'But you don't kill people just so that you can search their
rooms!'

'It depends how badly you want what you're after.'

Ken stopped. They had come abreast of the ferry departure point. He stood staring at the scene of bustling movement. Beyond the wooden jetty the disturbed water moved
restlessly. Along the lake the mountains were vaguely defined

humps looming in the darkness. The lights of villages at the lake shore resembled clusters of twinkling stars. Diana watched his profile, reluctant to break into his reverie.

'This place seems strangely familiar.' His voice was low. She could not tell whether he was talking to her or to himself. 'As if I'd been here before, in some other life.'

He stared away down the dark lake and she reflected again how much there could be in the past of a man his age that she would never know about.

'Come on,' he said at last, shaking off the mood. 'Let's turn back.'

A newspaper and magazine kiosk was still open, even at this late hour. Periodicals of many nationalities were on display, including many in English.

The vendor, his practised eye diagnosing the nationality of the passing couple, called out: 'Today's paper, sir.'

'No, thank you.' Ken had felt no wish to scrutinize the papers from home since that day in Venice when his eye had been caught by the report of the sex murder.

'You shivered. Are you feeling it cold?'

'No,' he said with perfect truth, and then followed up with a fib. 'I was just thinking back to that thief with the knife in Padua.'

'Do you still think that the thefts and the attacks are not connected?'

Ken shook his head. 'I'm not so sure now. Somehow realizing about that key makes me think there's a link, though we can't see what it is. Do you know what I thought of doing?'

'Tell me.'

'If I announced that I had found a key with the word Sablok on it the thief or the murderer might react in some way that would betray her – or them.'

'I hope you won't do anything so foolish, Ken. If you let it be known that you have the key you might not get off as lightly as Mr Benson did. We've only one more night and day and then we'll be home. Let's make the most of it.'

Yes, only one more night, Ken thought. And somehow I must get through it without revealing the claw marks on my chest.

There was rain on Como during the night and when the sun rose the mists were still veiling the upper slopes of the mountains. But during breakfast the warmth drew them gradually upwards until they dispersed in an unbroken blue sky. The weather promised to be brilliant for the last leg of the tour.

A whole day had passed now without any further incident and the mood of the party had lightened as if amongst the mountains they had found sanctuary from the threats which had hung over the cities of Lombardy. Gabriella was in as good spirits as anyone. Her colour was high and she had taken a lot of trouble with her make-up. She deliberately caught Ken's eye and gave a toss of her head which would not have shamed a thoroughbred racehorse.

Her party was already seated in the coach when the manager called her back into the hotel to take an urgent call from England.

It was Sammie and his voice sounded unusually subdued.

'Gabriella? You'd better prepare yourself for a shock. Mrs Rayburn's been found.'

'Yes?' Gabriella said guardedly. 'Is she all right?'

'She's dead. She's been dead five days.'

'Five days! That takes us back to the night we left Gatwick. Where has she been all this time?'

'Her body was hidden in the locker in the chaplain's office. The RC priest found her when he forced the lock to get at his surplice.'

'Of course. Today's Sunday. How on earth did anyone get her down to the chaplain's office? It's in the basement, near the toilets.'

'She must have walked down of her own free will. Whoever killed her must have thought up some plausible story to lure her down there. It probably wasn't hard. She was the sort of body who homes on clergymen.'

'They're sure she was deliberately killed?'

'The police won't say anything definite about that till after the inquest. That's fixed for later this morning. But if she wasn't, why stuff her body into the locker?'

Gabriella stared unseeingly at the graffiti on the wall of the telephone booth.

'Sammie.'

'Yes?'

'Have you told them about all the other things that have happened on this tour? About Miss Norman and Mrs Sloman and Mr Benson.'

'Yes. I felt I had to. The inspector is going to want to question everyone in your party. He was proposing to fly out but I explained to him that you'd all be back at Gatwick tonight. You'll find quite a reception committee.'

'I'd better tell them, hadn't I? Warn them to be prepared –'

'For God's sake, Gabriella! Not on your life. You must not breathe a word about this, not to anybody. Anybody, do you understand?'

'Yes, Sammie.'

'The inspector says carry on with today's tour as if nothing had happened and be sure you get to Turin in good time for the take-off. I'll make certain there's no delay this time. You should all be back here in – let's see – eleven hours from now.'

'Do the police think somebody in my party did it?'

'They're not telling me what they think. I wish I could come out and join you, Gabriella, but I'm tied here.'

'Oh, I'll manage,' Gabriella said, as bravely as she could. 'We're near the end of the road now.'

The coach wound its way northward along the western shore of Lake Como as far as the town of Argegno with its charming port, screened by a small jetty. From there it climbed the Valle d'Intelvi to Castiglione before dropping again to the shores of the Lake of Lugano, which it followed for thirty kilometres.

It was mid-morning as Joe swung away from the lake and dropped into bottom gear for the slow climb to Castel-vecchio a thousand feet above Lugano. The ancient castle, once a stronghold in the Guelph-Ghibelline wars, had been converted into a luxurious hotel. It was a regular stopping place for the tour, for its terraces and gardens, laid out behind the ancient battlements, provided the most wonderful views of the surrounding landscape.

The tyres of the coach crunched on gravel as it drew up at the entrance. Flower-beds and lawns sloped away to the forest below and well-tended paths led towards the steep escarpments on which the castle had been built. From the balconies and windows bougainvillaea tumbled in profusion.

'The place seems deserted!' Ken said, as Joe switched off his engine.

In the sudden silence Gabriella overheard his remark. There was a hint of secret daring or challenge in her face as she answered him.

'The hotel is only open in the full season. But we have a special arrangement. We always stop here for morning coffee.'

'Well, you couldn't have chosen a more beautiful spot,' Mrs Grant said. 'I will say that. Aren't those tea-roses, Dad? I didn't know they grew them in Italy.'

The party dismounted, gazing around them in slightly awed amazement at such sophistication combined with so much grandeur.

A waiter in a white coat had come to the front door. Gabriella walked over to speak to him, her movements as provocative as ever.

'*Buon giorno, signorina*. You are a little more early than usual today. The guests, they can wait a little quarter of an hour? You will have the coffee on the *terrazza*, as usual?'

'Not more than a quarter of an hour, Antonio,' Gabriella warned the young man sternly. 'We must be at Turin by four o'clock.'

'If there's a quarter of an hour to wait I'd like to powder my nose.' Mrs Jones, now attired in shocking-pink trousers, peered uncertainly through the very grandiose entrance. 'I wonder where the toilet is?'

'I'll come with you, Brenda,' Mrs Grant offered.

'What about you, Gareth?' Mr Grant said as the two ladies disappeared through the front door. 'Want to water the horses?'

'Naar!' exclaimed Gareth Jones scornfully. 'You go ahead if you want to. I'm going to look for a bush. If I know their little quarter of an hour it'll be a good thirty minutes.'

Gareth turned his broad and stocky back on the hesitating Mr Grant and chose a path that led out towards the old battlements and the ruins of what had been an outer fort. He hated everything about indoor lavatories, the shiny tiles, the hissing or squirting pipes of the urinals, the overpowering smell of disinfectant, the graffiti on the walls. He preferred to relieve himself in the open air, if possible at a spot which offered a good view.

Mr and Mrs Grant and Brenda had vanished into the hotel. The others were spreading out to explore the well-kept gardens. After several hours in the bus they all had an instinctive desire to get away on their own and have a few minutes of privacy. Tasker, again lugging his battery of equipment, was searching for a good vantage point to take a picture of the lake below. Benson was walking round the walls of the château, searching for indications of its age. The attractive Mrs Meredith had been strolling in the same direction, stopping frequently to examine some rare plant, but where the path divided she had taken another route. Gareth was soon screened by a plantation of young fir trees.

The path led him out on to the ancient battlements, whose foundations rested on the solid rock below. The terrace commanded a magnificent view of the surrounding hills and the lake. He threw a quick look to right and left, but he was well shielded by the young fir trees. The crack of a stick under weight and a faint rustle was probably some animal which had taken cover at his approach.

As soon as he had relieved himself he moved to one of the embrasures in the ancient wall. Looking at the sheer drop beyond, it was easy to imagine the defenders in times long past, shooting blunderbusses at their attackers or pouring boiling oil from the niches cut at regular intervals.

His reverie was broken by the quick rush of footsteps behind him. He only had time to half turn before the heavy lump of flint struck him on the temple.

CHAPTER VII

By the time the spruce waiter brought the coffee the entire party, with one exception, had settled themselves round the white wrought-iron tables on the open *terrazza*.

'What's Gareth up to, I wonder?' Mrs Jones said. 'I thought he was with you, Tom.'

'He went off to – to –' Mr Grant stammered into silence, glancing nervously at Miss Foxell.

'Oh, I know what he went to do, but he doesn't usually take as long as this. Does anyone mind if I give him a call?'

Nobody raised an objection as Mrs Jones went to the edge of the terrace and filled her considerable lungs.

'Gareth!' she called in a voice that had been trained from childhood in the Aberkegir Colliery Choir. 'Gareth!'

Her voice echoed back from the woods across the valley. Sundry birds and small beasties broke from cover in panic.

'That'll bring him,' Mrs Jones stated with confidence and sat down to her coffee.

Ten minutes later, as Gabriella was beginning to look at her watch, Mrs Jones was showing the first signs of concern.

'It's not like him,' she said to Mrs Grant, then turned to Gabriella. 'Ask your driver to give a few blasts on his horn, love. He may have wandered on and not noticed the time.'

Gabriella nodded and crossed the gravel drive to the coach, on whose step Joe was sitting, drinking his own coffee. A moment later a series of trumpet calls on the set of Alpine horns echoed round the hills.

'I don't like this,' Mrs Jones said, when another five minutes had passed. 'He's been gone a good half-hour now. Did anyone see where he went exactly? Mrs Grant and I were in the hotel.'

'I saw him going off along the path towards the battle-ments,' Diana said. 'He seemed in quite a hurry.'

'I can confirm that,' Benson's spectacles glinted as he nodded. 'I was making a study of the stonework of the building. I went across to the fort later but I didn't see him.'

'We came back from the fort along the battlements, didn't we, Jean? But there was no sign of him there.'

Mr Grant nodded towards Tasker, who was putting a new film in his camera. 'You didn't see him, Tasker? I saw you setting up your easel over by the geraniums.'

'Tripod,' Tasker corrected him. 'No, I didn't see Mr Jones after he went along that path.'

Ken got to his feet. There had been something ominous about the complete silence which had followed Brenda Jones's call and the peal of the Alpine horns. 'Let's have a look round. Mr Grant, could you check that he's not some-where in the hotel? Benson, perhaps you would try round the other side of the house. Tasker and I can try these paths leading round the battlements.'

Tasker, slightly resentful of the way Ken had taken charge of the situation, asserted his authority when the two men came to a place where the path divided.

'You take the left-hand path and I'll take the right,' he said. 'They may meet at the other end.'

'Good idea,' Ken agreed equably.

He had gone along the path about fifty yards when it emerged on the terrace flanking the battlements. He slowed, compelled to admire the view despite the strong premonition which was growing in him. It was not much farther on that he saw that the gravel of the path had been scuffed up.

He put his hands on the parapet, leaned through one of the embrasures and stared down. The spreadeagled form a long way below looked like a bundle of bloodstained rags. A *frisson* ran through him, an urgent sense of danger. He pulled back from the parapet, turned round quickly.

Tasker had come along the path from the other direction and was a few paces away.

K

'No sign of him here,' he said.

'I've found him.' Ken's voice was not much better than a croak.

'You've found him? Where is he, then?'

Ken nodded towards the parapet. 'Down there.'

'He went down and now I suppose he can't find a way up,' Tasker suggested unsympathetically.

'You'd better look for yourself.'

Tasker for the first time tumbled to the fact that something terrible had happened. He went past Ken, leaned over the parapet and then turned back rapidly.

'My God!' He had begun to breathe fast. 'Is he dead?'

'He must be, to judge by the way he's lying. No one could survive a fall from this height on to rocks. We must get back quickly, prevent Mrs Jones from seeing this.'

But it was not Mrs Jones they met, running along the path towards them. Waiting on the *terrazza* Diana had become aware that Ken had gone out on to the old battlements alone with Alan Tasker, and the memory of that moment on Monte Baldo swept over her.

'Oh Ken! There you are!'

She saw that the relief which she had been unable to conceal had passed unnoticed. Ken's face was set and pale.

'Diana, something's happened. He fell from the parapet. I don't know how the hell we can get down to him but you've got to prevent Mrs Jones from coming along here. And can you tell her – can you break it to her – ?'

'He's dead, you mean?'

'He must be. I can't see how he could have survived that fall.'

They looked at each other and had to pass the message without words. They were very conscious that Tasker was standing a few feet away.

'Tasker, could you tell Gabriella? She'll have to send for an ambulance and they may need rescue equipment. I'm going to try and find a way of getting down to him.'

'You will be careful, won't you, Ken?'

'Yes,' he promised. 'I'll be careful.'

It all took a very long time. Ken found a gate at the top of a flight of steps which led down to the steeply sloping, pine-clad slopes below the old fortress. Gareth Jones's body lay away to his right across rocks where normally nobody in their senses ventured.

It took him twenty minutes under the hot sun to reach the spot and by the time he did so he was bathed in sweat. There was no possibility that Gareth Jones could have survived that fall. He had bounced off a number of rocks and suffered multiple injuries to his head and body before coming to rest where he now lay. The gay straw hat had lodged against a stone a dozen yards away.

Ken was glad he had come down. He was able to keep the swarming insects off the body and perform one last act of friendship by pulling up the open zip on Gareth Jones's flies.

It was another half-hour before the ambulance crew arrived and another forty minutes before the stretcher was hauled by a winch up to the parapet seventy feet above. By the time Ken had made his way back across the rocks and mounted the steps the ambulance had disappeared.

As he crossed the gravel drive to the front of the hotel Brenda Jones came out of the door to meet him. Her face was grey, her features numbed by shock. There was no sign of tears, but rather a strange dignity mingled with something else – perhaps anger, or resolution.

'I'd like to see where he fell, Mr Forsythe. Will you take me there?'

Beyond her he could see Mrs Grant hovering helplessly and a very tense Gabriella. He was about to try and talk her out of what was sure to be a distressing experience but another look at her face changed his mind.

'If you want. It's along that path.'

He started to walk slowly beside her in that direction. Mrs Grant tagged in behind.

'I don't want a crowd,' Brenda Jones told her, and Ken

guessed that she had found 'Mum's' attempts at consolation hard to bear.

Mrs Grant stifled a sob and turned back, deeply hurt.

Ken took her along the path, on to the terrace bordered by the parapet and stopped at the embrasure.

'Here?' she said.

He nodded.

She went and stood, staring out over the lake to the mountains beyond.

'Trust you to choose a lovely spot like this, Gareth. I wonder where are you now?'

He stayed because he was afraid that her icy control might break. She remained as motionless as a statue. Never once did she look downward at the rocks below.

At last she turned round, putting a lifetime behind her.

'Of course he never fell. Gareth was pushed over. I know that.'

Ken made no comment. They walked back to the hotel in silence. Gabriella, who had been sitting in the coach talking to Joe, stepped down to meet her.

'That was no accident,' Mrs Jones said to her. 'Gareth was killed on purpose. I want the police called and this tour's not moving on till they've found out who did it.'

Gabriella, now almost as strained and pale as the bereaved woman, nodded her head, accepting what had become inevitable.

'The *carabinieri* have already been notified,' she told Brenda Jones. 'They'll be sending someone up after lunch.'

The manager of the hotel had gone off for the day but the young waiter and the cook managed to put up a scratch lunch which the members of the party helped to carry out to the terrace. Even the two Preston kids, strangely cowed and silent, helped with the task. Gabriella had managed to persuade Mrs Jones to have hers quietly in one of the hotel rooms which had been opened up specially.

While they were eating, two uniformed *carabinieri* arrived in a small Fiat. They insisted on Joe parking the coach on the avenue at the back of the hotel and confiscated the ignition key. They made no attempt to question any of the members of the party but stationed themselves ostentatiously at the *porte cochère* which was the only exit.

'We seem to have been placed under guard,' Mr Benson commented, eyeing the uniformed men anxiously.

'They're only *carabinieri*,' Gabriella said scornfully. 'They're not capable of carrying out an investigation. They're only here to see that no one leaves before the inspector from the Questura in Varese gets here.'

'He's certainly taking his time,' Mr Grant remarked.

'Before he does get here,' Ken suggested, 'don't you think we ought to take stock of our position? A lot of things have happened but we've never discussed it openly.'

'What do you mean exactly?' Tasker wanted to know. Everyone else had stopped talking and was listening.

'Well, since the tour began we have had two deaths and one accident which nearly proved fatal. We have had at least one violent assault and a number of people's rooms have been rifled. And we know that Mrs Rayburn has not been seen since we left Gatwick. It seems to me the truth must be faced that all this is not just coincidence or bad luck. It has something to do with this tour and the people on it. Now, the Italian police will be here any minute and all this is going to come out. That means they'll be checking back with their colleagues in Como, Milan, Verona, Padua, Venice and probably eventually England. God knows how long that will take and my guess is that we shall not be allowed to leave here till they've completed their enquiries.'

A stunned silence followed Ken's statement. He was watching carefully the faces turned towards him. The Grants looked alarmed and frightened, the two Preston children intrigued, Jim and Jean detached in a world of their own. Benson was nodding his agreement, while Tasker still wore his resentful expression. Miss Foxell gazed at the distant hills, whilst Doreen Wilkins stared at him with a brittle intensity.

'However, it's quite possible,' Ken went on, 'that we have the means to find the solution ourselves. Can we cast our thoughts back to that evening at Gatwick? Did anyone notice anything unusual about Mrs Rayburn – what she did, what she said, who spoke to her? Think back hard.'

After a moment Mr Preston cleared his throat nervously. 'Well, we were sitting in the same part of the hall, in that sort of three-sided square behind the pillars.'

He looked round as if hesitating to put the finger on any of his fellow tourists.

'Mr and Mrs Jones were there too and Mr Benson, and I think, if I remember rightly, that Mrs Meredith was sitting beside Mrs Rayburn.'

'Yes, I was,' Diana confirmed.

'Alice and I were in that part,' Doreen Wilkins said. 'As well as Mrs Sloman and Mrs Hayward. Even before this business today I'd worked out that all three people who've been attacked since we left England were in that group with Mrs Rayburn. Now, with Mr Jones that makes four.'

To which you can add one more, Ken thought. But it would seem a bit odd to mention the Padua incident at this late stage.

'And what about the burglaries?' Mrs Grant asked, holding tightly on to her husband's arm.

A blue Alfa-Romeo had come in through the *porte-cochère*, eliciting a salute from the two uniformed *carabinieri*. It swept to a halt at the front of the hotel and a surprisingly young man in a natty mustard-coloured suit stepped out.

'Well, let's see whose room was entered,' Ken began to tick the names off on his fingers. 'The Prestons', Mrs Meredith's, Mr Benson's, the Joneses' if you count their suitcases. That's all, but they were in the same group at Gatwick.'

He was watching the new arrival, who had strolled over to confer with the *carabinieri*.

'You see, we're getting somewhere already. It's a pity,

but I'm afraid we're not going to be able to continue this discussion much longer. But if any of you think of anything that happened during that period of waiting which might have a meaning I suggest you come and tell me.'

'Would it not be more proper to report it to the police?' Tasker objected.

'As you like. It's just that I'm not quite sure what their attitude will be.'

'You mean we're all suspects,' Doreen Wilkins said.

'To them we certainly are.'

Suddenly Miss Foxell detached her sad blue eyes from the distant hills and made one of her very rare statements.

'You intend to establish that some member of this party is a thief and a murderer?'

Ken was wondering how to parry the question when Jim Collins spoke up.

'Of course, there was that plainclothes policeman. You remember, asking Gabriella if she could identify all her party.'

'He said it was because of pickpockets and so on,' Benson said. 'But I wonder now if it could have been something else.'

'It was.' Gabriella had stood up and was nervously awaiting the young man in the yellow suit, who was now approaching. 'But it had nothing to do with us. Someone had telephoned to say there was a bomb in the airport. It was obviously a hoax but they had to check.'

'A bomb in the airport!' exclaimed Mrs Grant. 'Whatever will they think of next?'

The young man had come to the edge of the terrace and was surveying the group. He gave the impression of being very resentful that his lunch had been interrupted by the behaviour of this party of itinerant tourists.

'Is anyone in charge here?' he demanded in Italian.

'I am the courier,' Gabriella answered in the same language and went across to where he was standing.

The inspector's eyes raked her with undisguised sensuality.

'You are Italian?'

'I was born in Italy, but I live in England.'

'*Bene*. You can act as interpreter in my preliminary investigation. But first I want a word with you.'

He drew her away and they conversed for a while in quick-fire Italian while the party watched anxiously. When Gabriella came back she seemed subdued and worried.

'He says he wants you all inside the hotel and no one is to come out without permission. Mr Forsythe, would you come and show him where you found the – where you found Mr Jones?'

While the others straggled protestingly towards the hotel, Ken, the inspector and Gabriella walked along the path towards the battlements. Ken attempted a few words of conversation but the Italian, who had identified himself as Inspector Carlomaria Ponti, made it clear that he was not interested in anything Ken had to say, except in answer to his questions.

They stopped at the embrasure, where the ground was now well scuffed up by the rescue operation.

'It was here?'

Ponti stared round him, then switched his dark eyes to Ken.

'It was you who found the body? You understand the question?'

'Yes,' Ken answered in Italian.

'How did you know where to look?'

'When Mr Jones had been missing for some time we organized a little search party. It just happened that I was doing this area.'

'Who organized the search party?'

'I did.'

'You did. Have you some official standing in this touring group?'

'No. But nobody else was helping much so I thought I'd give a lead.'

'So you organized the search and arranged it so that you

would find the body yourself?'

'It just happened that way,' Ken answered patiently. He was beginning to wish he had let Gabriella do the interpreting. This way the Italian had the advantage of him. But he was frankly surprised at his hostile approach. 'As a matter of fact it was Tasker who asked me to take this path.'

'Tasker?'

'Mr Tasker,' Gabriella chipped in, 'is another member of the party.'

Ponti nodded. 'How did you know exactly where to look for the body?'

'I saw that the ground just here was scuffed up and something made me think of looking over the parapet.'

'Something? What thing?'

'Well, a premonition, I suppose. A suspicion that he'd had an accident.'

'An accident? But I understand the charge has been made that he was murdered.'

'That's what his wife believes.'

'But you do not believe that?'

Ken reflected before replying. He was well aware that the sharp little eyes were reading his face as he hesitated. This man might be young but he had a mind like a ferret.

'I think it would be very hard to fall from there accidentally. And besides, there have been other incidents.'

'There have been other incidents?' The detective tapped his teeth with his pen and half closed his eyes. 'We will come back to that. Now I want you to tell me exactly what you observed.'

Ken gave as close an account as he could of what he had seen when he looked through the embrasure.

'So what did you do then?'

'I asked Mr Tasker to send for an ambulance and Mrs Meredith to break it to Mrs Jones.'

'Mrs Meredith is also a member of the group?'

'Yes,' Gabriella confirmed tersely and her mouth tightened.

'What was the purpose of your going down to the body? That must have been a very difficult climb.'

'There are steps farther along, leading down to the forest. But I agree it was not easy. Still, there was a faint chance that he might still have been alive, and in any case there had to be someone down there when the ambulance men came.'

'I see. Did you touch the body?'

'Only to do up the flies.'

'Why did you do that? To the dead such things are not important.'

'Yes, I know. I can only say that to me it was important.'

'You mentioned other incidents. Will you please tell me about them?'

Ken turned to Gabriella and said in English: 'I don't know that it's proper for me to make a statement about what's been happening. It really ought to come from you in your official capacity.'

Gabriella translated the gist of what Ken had said. The inspector listened, staring at the ground.

'As the signore raised the point I would like him to answer the question.'

'Can I say it in English and let the signorina translate as I go along?'

Ponti shrugged his shoulders. 'It will take longer, but if you prefer it that way . . .'

Choosing his words carefully Ken told him what had befallen Mrs Rayburn, Alice Norman and Mrs Sloman, and the various thefts or attempted thefts.

'There's something else that Mr Forsythe does not know,' Gabriella said hesitantly when Ken had finished. 'It is true about Mrs Rayburn disappearing, but I heard from our tour operator this morning that she may have been murdered. Her body was found in the chaplain's office at Gatwick Airport five days after we left there.'

'You've kept very quiet about that,' Ken said accusingly. 'It throws a completely different light on – '

'Sammie told me to keep the information to myself,' she flashed back angrily, 'and I don't see any reason why I should take you into my confidence.'

'Just a moment.' Ponti had been watching their faces with his intent expression. He held up his hand to quench the sudden flare-up of emotion. 'The British police have been informed, of course?'

'Yes. There was to be an inquest this morning. They will decide whether it is a case of murder or not.'

'Just to recapitulate,' Ponti said. 'The first incident was at Gatwick, the second at Venezia, the third at Verona and the fourth here. And there were thefts at Venezia, Padova and Milano.'

'Yes. And actually there was one other incident.'

'Oh?'

'Yes. In Padua.' Ken could see Gabriella out of the corner of his eye. He knew what her reaction would be but to suppress evidence now would be too dangerous. 'I was in Mrs Meredith's room until fairly late that night. Someone opened the door with a pass key and came in. The lights were out so I could only see a vague shape. When I challenged the figure it came at me with a knife. My arm was slashed rather badly and I'm afraid I let them get away.'

Ponti was evaluating Ken's statement thoughtfully. He knew that Gabriella was glaring at him but he could not bring himself to look round at her.

'With a knife?' Ponti repeated, shaking his head dubiously. 'You reported this, of course?'

'No.'

'Why not? If you knew there had already been other thefts.'

'I had this bad cut on my arm and by the time that had been attended to there was not much point in raising a hue and cry.'

'Just how many of these incidents have been reported to the police?'

Ken now glanced at Gabriella but she was standing apart, looking back towards the hotel and he could see that he wouldn't get any more help from that quarter.

'Well, I'd like to remind you that I'm just a tourist on this trip like everyone else so I'm not in any position to speak officially. But, as I understand it, the British police were informed of the disappearance of Mrs Rayburn at Gatwick. I presume, since Miss Norman died in hospital, that the authorities in Venice were informed. The police were certainly on the scene soon after Mrs Sloman's accident and they were called in again at Milan when Mr Benson was knocked on the head and tied up.'

Ponti raised his eyebrows and addressed Gabriella.

'Under such circumstances, signorina, I am astonished that you continued with this tour. Or do the English regard such a succession of crimes as perfectly normal?'

'I discussed it with my tour operator,' Gabriella explained with a touch of desperation. 'He advised me to carry on. You see, although rooms were entered nothing was stolen and for a time it looked as if these accidents were just bad luck.'

'It is bad luck,' Ponti said acidly, 'that you have to bring your coach-load of trouble to Varese. I can see that I'm going to have a lot of work to do. You can be thankful that your murderer chose such a beautiful spot, because I think you will all be here for some time.'

The afternoon was interminable. The time would have passed more agreeably if they had been able to go out into the gardens and enjoy the sunshine. Instead they had to sit in a hotel which was working on a drastically reduced staff, and where none of the services on which guests rely to pass the time were available.

Soon after Ken had been released by Ponti, with a warning that he would be questioned again, another car-load of plainclothes men arrived and disappeared with their cameras and cases of equipment in the direction of the battlements.

The manager of the hotel, who had been summoned by the waiter from his town apartment in Varese, arrived at about four and spread his arms in a gesture of crucified despair when he heard that he was required to accommodate seventeen unwanted guests at the police's pleasure. But when he had vented his lamentations on the long-suffering Gabriella he clapped his hands for action and got to work organizing food and opening up bedrooms. A bargain had been struck and Connoisseur Tours would pay double tariff because of the inconvenience caused.

Not long after that Ponti came into the hotel and called for a beer. While he drank it he studied the passenger list which he had required Gabriella to provide. Then he installed himself in the manager's private office and began the long process of questioning each member of the party.

'He's a little demon,' Ken warned Diana, 'and very much on the ball. I had to tell him about that business in Padua, so don't be surprised if he asks you about it.'

'Did you say anything about the key? The Sablok key.'

'No. I didn't. I'm wondering whether I ought to when he questions me again, but something makes me hesitate. If it was the British police I'd feel different, but this little man's so very hostile. He seems to take it as a personal affront that an English crime has been dumped in his lap.'

'Mrs Meredith.' Gabriella was crossing the lounge from the direction of the manager's office. The expression on her face was ominous. 'Signor Ponti wants to see you next.'

As Ken watched the two women walk away his feelings were mixed. It was the first time he had seen them together on their own and that made him slightly uncomfortable. Gabriella had put on her most provocative expression and Ken reflected with alarm that all Diana's replies could be given a slant by her translations.

The two Preston children were just coming back from

the ping-pong room. As they slumped down beside their parents with the listless manner of teenagers bored beyond endurance, Ken realized that this was a unique opportunity to talk to the Prestons on their own. They had made their headquarters in an alcove at the end of the lounge. The other tourists were tactfully leaving them strictly to themselves.

Ken walked over to join them under the impassive scrutiny of Nigel and Emma.

'Mind if I join you?'

'No, please do,' Preston said. He was still wearing the baggy shorts which he considered suitable attire in a hot climate. 'We're wondering when we're going to be grilled by the little man.'

'He's taking a lot of time over it,' Ken said. 'At this rate he'll still be on the job by midnight.'

'Well, I'm not letting these children stay up as late as that,' declared Mrs Preston, 'not for any police inspector.'

'Oh, *Mother*!' Emma protested in disgust. She squirmed farther back into the chair and doubled her knees up to put her feet on the edge.

'It just struck me,' Ken said, pulling his chair a little farther forward so that he would not have to speak so loudly, 'that all four of you were in that group where Mrs Rayburn was sitting. It was a pity we had to stop that discussion we were having on the terrace. We were just starting to get somewhere.'

'You mean that plainclothes man who came round? But signorina said it was to do with some warning about a bomb.'

'The detective said it was to do with thieves,' Emma said. 'We know there's a thief somewhere in this party, don't we, Pop? And what's more he's still got my camel-skin belt. At least I'm sure that's what happened to it.'

'Were you all there when the detective came? Did you notice anyone reacting strangely?'

'Pop and I had gone off to get the meal vouchers,' Nigel

said. 'They'd just made that announcement on the loud-speakers. We wanted to beat the queue.'

'That's right, dear!' Mrs Preston was regarding with admiration this son with the phenomenal memory. 'Emma and I stayed behind while you and Daddy went off. Isn't that right, Emma?'

Emma nodded.

'I suppose you don't remember who else was there when the detective came?'

'There was Mrs Sloman.' Emma uncoiled her legs, put her feet on the floor and leaned forward with her elbows on her knees. She would be quite attractive, Ken thought, when those spots had gone away. 'I remember because she kept looking at my rings. Probably imagined I was engaged to some oil sheik. Mrs Meredith was there. I knew she was Mrs something and I was trying to make out if she had a husband. She was sitting beside Mrs Rayburn and being very nice to her.'

'Go on,' Ken prompted. 'You've obviously got a very good memory.'

'Mrs Jones made Mr Jones stay put while she went to get the vouchers. I think they took turns to do things and he'd queued for the other voucher – the orangeade one. Miss Norman was there and Mr Benson. He was sitting on the other side of Mrs Rayburn. He'd just been to the gents and one of his fly-buttons was showing.'

'Emma!'

'There's nothing wrong about fly-buttons, Mother! Girls have them now. There's nothing secret about fly-buttons any more. *Honestly*!'

Ken detached himself from the family wrangle. They had apparently not noticed the significant fact which had emerged from Emma's reconstruction. Of the eight people who had been in that corner of the Main Hall when the detective had paid his visit six had been the victims of attacks, three of them fatal. The reason why Emma and Mrs Preston had escaped might be because the Prestons were usually all together, a fact which afforded them a kind of protection.

'It doesn't seem to make any kind of sense, does it?' Preston said as Ken stood up.

'None at all. But I hope you won't take it amiss if I make a suggestion. It's that you keep together, all four of you. Above all, I wouldn't let your wife or daughter be left on their own.'

'Good God!' Preston shook his head as if cold water had been poured over his short-back-and-sides hair. 'Who'd want to harm them?'

'Who'd want to harm Mrs Rayburn, or Alice Norman, or Gareth Jones?'

He left them to work that one out and went to the bar near the main entrance which had been opened by the small waiter who had served them coffee. Diana was still in the manager's office with the detective.

Ken had time to consume a couple of long Campari sodas before the door of the office was opened. He caught a glimpse of Ponti seated at the desk with a uniformed *carabiniera* beside him. Diana and Gabriella came out of the office together, the former very white in the face. As soon as she saw Ken she veered in his direction.

'I really am sorry about that, Mrs Meredith,' Gabriella was saying. 'But I *had* to translate those questions. It made me feel extremely embarrassed.'

'It wasn't your fault.' Diana forced a smile at the younger woman. 'I suppose he has to do his job.'

'Yes, but if I'd known it was going to be like that I'd never have agreed to interpret.'

'You look as if you could do with a drink,' Ken said. 'What'll you have?'

'Something strong. Do they have gin here?'

'We'll soon find out. For you, Gabriella?'

To his relief Gabriella shook her head.

'Thanks, but I have to find Miss Wilkins. She's next on the list.'

'So, what was all that about?' Ken asked, when the barman had mixed a strong dry Martini according to his instructions.

'I seem to be Inspector Ponti's prime suspect. He practically accused me of pushing Mr Jones over the edge.'

'But that's preposterous! I thought I was the one he suspected. What was your motive supposed to be?'

Diana took a sip from her drink. 'Motive didn't come into it. But you see I was apparently the only person who has admitted to having been near the battlements when it must have happened.'

'What about the other killings? Are you supposed to have poisoned Alice Norman? You couldn't have pushed Mrs Sloman under that car, because we were together when it happened.'

'I'm not sure that he's going to believe that. The fact that we didn't report the thief, or murderer, coming into my room in Padua counts against us. I think he believes that we just invented that to divert suspicion.'

Ken shook his head in disbelief. Gabriella was just crossing the hall with Doreen Wilkins. He watched them disappear into the office and a horrifying suspicion grew in his mind.

'Gabriella had to translate all your replies as well as the questions?'

'Yes. The inspector didn't speak any English.'

'Do you think she might have twisted your answers? Made them sound a bit more incriminating?'

Diana stared at the closed door, her brow furrowed. 'No, I don't think she could have. Anyway I'm sure she wouldn't do anything like that. She may be jealous but she's not vicious.'

If you could see my chest, Ken thought, you might not be so confident about that.

The meal which was served that evening had mostly come out of tins. The atmosphere in the dining-room was tense. The brutally direct methods of the inspector had made

L

every member of the party feel that they were in some way responsible. More than that, the knowledge that one of their number was undoubtedly a murderer made each little group suspicious of the others.

After a short interval, during which Ponti snatched a quick meal in the office, the series of interrogations continued. Ken had been not far wrong in his forecast that they would last till midnight. It was after ten when Miss Foxell, the last to be questioned, came out of the office. Another half-hour passed before Ponti himself emerged. Ken did not know whether to take it as a good or a bad sign that he was not called for further questioning.

The Italian instructed Gabriella to assemble all her party, including Joe, in the dining-room and when they were ready strode to the head of the room. Gabriella again had to act as interpreter and translate the terse statement.

'I have now completed my preliminary interrogations. It seems evident to me that the crime committed here today was the last of a series which should have been reported long ago. I hold all of you responsible for failure to report these felonies to the police. I now have to confer with my colleagues in London, Venezia, Padova, Verona, Milano and Como. This will take some time. Meanwhile you are confined to the hotel, all of you. And I must warn you that the *carabinieri* will be on guard and I cannot answer for the consequences if my orders are ignored.'

In the stunned silence which followed Ken clearly heard Tasker swallowing saliva.

It was Benson who had the nerve to speak up. 'How long do you intend to keep us here in these conditions? I'm not sure what the law is here but in England you could not hold us without bringing specific charges.'

Ponti listened with mock politeness while Gabriella translated. His answer was brief.

'This is *not* England. How long you remain here will depend on the decision of my superiors. That might very well be that you should all be moved to the prison in Varese.'

When Gabriella had translated he asked her to enquire if there were any other questions.

There were none.

'It's like being back at school,' Benson protested as they all trooped out into the hall. 'Someone in the class is naughty and everyone has to be punished till the culprit owns up – or gets caught.'

'I think he's just some junior official who's overplaying his hand,' Preston stated. 'He's not sure what to do and he's trying to bluff his way through by being so aggressive.'

'Don't you think we ought to call in the nearest British Consul?' It was Tasker who made the suggestion. 'I mean, we've got to protect our rights. I know I've got an important meeting in Bristol the day after tomorrow.'

'I've been on the phone to Mr Sampson.' Gabriella had overheard these comments. 'He's promised to get in touch with the Foreign Office and see that we get proper legal aid. In the meantime his advice is to play it cool and do what the Italians say.'

'Thanks very much,' Jim muttered to Jean. 'Cooped up here with a dozen possible murderers.'

'I suppose Jim's right,' Ken said to Diana as they sat in a corner of the deserted bar with the last drinks that had been served before it closed down. 'If you eliminate the impossibles that does leave a dozen.'

'Who are the impossibles?'

'Well, Mrs Jones for a start. Benson, because he was a victim. Doreen Wilkins, because she would not have poisoned her friend. Who does that leave?'

'Miss Foxell, Jim and Jean, Mr and Mrs Preston –'

'And their kids.'

'You count them?'

'You count everybody.'

'Then I suppose we have to include Mr and Mrs Grant.' Diana was counting the names on her fingers. 'And Mr Tasker. That's ten.'

'You've forgotten us,' Ken reminded her.

'But we can rule you and me out.'

'Maybe. But the others don't. And Inspector Ponti most certainly doesn't. I don't like the way this is going, and I don't share Preston's view that the little man is overplaying his hand.'

Ken stretched his arm to run the sleeve back and look at his watch.

'Do you realize that we were due back at Gatwick half an hour ago? If this hadn't happened we might have discovered the reason for all this by now.'

'You mean the key?'

'Yes. More and more I feel that it's in some extraordinary way the cause of all this.'

'And you still haven't mentioned it?'

'Something stops me. If I could just hand it to the CID man in charge of the Rayburn case I'd do so like a shot. It's the only possible explanation for Mrs Rayburn's murder and it offers the only possible explanation for these other incidents. Somebody is feverishly searching for that key and gradually trying to eliminate all the people who were in Mrs Rayburn's group. Don't ask me why. The answer is in that locker at Gatwick. I'm sure of it.'

Diana glanced over her shoulder at the door, just to make sure no one was standing there listening. 'Could you send it back to the CID by express post?'

'And entrust it to the Italian postal services? They're on strike more often than not.'

Ken finished his drink and stubbed his cigarette on the tray. Out in the hall someone was extinguishing lights. Most of the party had gone off to their rooms, taking good care to lock themselves in. The hotel was settling down for an uneasy night.

'There's only one way to make absolutely sure of it,

Diana. That's to go back to Gatwick myself and find out what's in the locker.'

'How are you going to get away from here with the police on guard?'

'I'm going to take the bus. I can coast it down the hill till I'm clear of the place.'

'But what about – You said you couldn't bring yourself to drive a car. That the doctors had warned you not to try.'

'I've got to beat that,' Ken said tersely. To her alarm she saw that even as he spoke small beads of sweat were forming on his brow. 'I've just got to beat it.'

'Now remember. Don't open your door to anyone, anyone at all, until it's broad daylight. And tomorrow stay close to the others. Don't let yourself get caught like you did with Tasker. If you do get into trouble, ask Benson. He's a bit of an old woman but he's the only man we can be certain is not the criminal.'

'You're sure this is the best way, Ken? Everyone's going to take your disappearance as an admission of guilt.'

'We've been over all that. By mid-morning tomorrow I'll have seen the CID, hopefully with some conclusive evidence.'

It was a little after one a.m. For the past hour Ken had been watching the gardens below, locating the *carabinieri* guards and noting the pattern of their movements. He had come to the conclusion that they spent most of the time smoking in one of the sun lounges, and so there would not be much difficulty in eluding them. Ponti was probably relying more on his threats than on his guards to discourage anyone who might decide to pack up and go home to the UK.

Ken checked his pockets to make sure he had the Sablok key, his currency and credit card, his passport, the length of wire he had cut from the lead to the bedside light. He signalled to Diana to switch off the lights then opened the window of her room. The garden lay twenty feet below, its shrubs and flower-beds vaguely visible under the light of the stars.

No sign of movement.

'Goodbye,' he whispered.

'Goodbye, darling. Please be careful.'

There was enough creeper to make the climb down to the ground simple. Once on the grass he stood for a minute, just in case the *carabinieri* were on the prowl. When he looked up he could see the white blob of her face at the window.

He gave a wave to show that all was well, then began to skirt the house, keeping close to the shadow of the walls. To avoid the open lawns at the back he made a wide detour through low bushes to reach the avenue of cypresses leading to the hotel's rear entrance. It was there that the coach had been parked.

When he reached it he saw with relief that it was pointing downhill. To coast out in reverse would have been possible, but very much more difficult, especially as it was almost pitch dark in the shadow of the cypresses.

His eyes had accustomed themselves to the darkness sufficiently for him to find the handle of the sliding door beside the driver's seat. He eased it back gently and climbed in.

Immediately a knot seemed to form in his stomach and the familiar paralysis gripped his body. He willed his hands to grasp the steering wheel but they refused to move. His feet, instead of feeling for the pedals, were clamped uselessly to the floor. He gritted his teeth, felt the cold sweat breaking out on his body, heard the roaring beginning in his ears. The urge to escape from the driving seat was becoming irresistible. Beyond the huge windscreen the moonlit avenue dimmed as his vision clouded. If he didn't get out he would scream . . .

Then a sound of voices broke through his frenzy from the world of reality. The roaring sound faded as some animal instinct banished his delirium. He froze, listening.

The two *carabinieri* had decided to make one of their intermittent patrols. They were passing on the other side of the line of cypresses, not ten yards away. He waited, feeling sure that an inspection of the coach must be included in their rounds.

But the voices faded and died altogether as they moved round to the other side of the château. Now was his chance.

He had put his foot on the brake pedal, slipped the gear lever into neutral and carefully released the hand-brake before he realized that his hands and legs were at last obeying his brain. The moment of danger, the knowledge that he could not go back to Diana and admit failure, had proved stronger than the old subconscious fears.

He eased his pressure on the foot-brake and the coach began to move slowly forward. Luckily there was no gravel here and the tyres made only a slight noise. The gradient was fairly gentle. Mastering a sudden renewal of panic, he reminded himself that he had to build up enough speed to carry him over the gentle slope just before the opening on to the public road. Without the ignition key he could not start the engine.

Steering by watching the tops of the trees against the sky, he felt his speed rise till he judged it must be about twenty miles an hour. In the dark it seemed more like fifty. Then he met the upward gradient and felt all the momentum he had built up gradually dissipate itself. If the coach stopped now he would have no alternative but to abandon it and climb back into the hotel. He would just have to accept that as the decision of fate.

The speed had dropped to walking pace as the vehicle gently coasted over the top of the rise, passed between the pillars flanking the entrance and reached the road. Ken swung right on to the hill up which they had come fourteen hours before. Without power assistance on the steering it took all his strength to spin the big wheel.

He coasted for half a mile, keeping his speed in check with the hand-brake because he knew that there was down gradient now as far as the lake below. When a particularly acute bend took him out of sight of the hotel he switched on the lights. The road ahead was abruptly flooded with almost dazzling light from the six headlamps.

He let the speed build up and nearly met disaster at the next bend. The coach, unlike a car, had no self-centring action and had to be deliberately steered out of the corner on to a straight line. Negotiating the series of bends was harder work than he had thought. Normally the driver had the assistance of the hydraulic servo system to swing the big Fiat through the curves. Ken found that it took all his strength to turn the broad nine-inch-wide wheels. His legs were working as hard as his arms for, with a dead engine, he had no servo assistance on the brakes either. Nor could he build engine revolutions to get into a low gear and of course he was deprived of the usual braking effect of compression.

And the gradient was getting steeper.

After less than a mile he realized that he was being carried down the hill by a runaway vehicle. The bends were now rushing at him with frightening speed. He had to keep his head and choose the best line for each corner. Even so the twin sets of rear tyres swung out on to the verge as the Fiat, rocking dangerously, lurched first to the left then to the right. The effect of the sideways friction scrubbed away some of his speed, but it only built up again as thirteen thousand kilograms of metal gathered fresh impetus.

Ken knew that he was faced by a totally new driving experience. In ordinary circumstances this vehicle was a docile creature obedient to the power-assisted systems. On a steep gradient without its engine it seemed more like an aircraft diving out of control. With its long wheelbase and six well-treaded tyres it could not be tweaked and bounced round corners like a rally car. Only sheer brute force could keep it on the road.

He began to pray that nothing was coming up the hill. The descent seemed interminable, the bends innumerable.

Again and again the branches of trees slashed the roof as
he swung wide on to the verges. The worst moment was
when he saw a hairpin ahead, beyond which was a black
void. Only a low barrier separated the road from the
precipice beyond. The slope was so steep here that he could
not lose speed. He spun the big horizontal wheel with all his
strength, felt his body tipped sideways by centrifugal force.
Half-way through the bend he knew he was not going to
make it. The low barrier disappeared under the front of
the bus. His headlamps swept empty air, below him was
blackness. Though he expected at any instant to feel the
coach topple over the edge some instinct to survive kept him
holding the wheel on full lock.

Then, miraculously, leaves and branches swept the windscreen, the headlamps swung round and there was the road
ahead of him again. The front wheels, set six feet to the
rear of his seat, had remained on the road while his seat
had hung over the abyss.

He was sweating profusely and his arms and legs were
aching with fatigue when at last the hill levelled off slightly
and he saw the lights of the lakeside village ahead.

He managed to stop by the first of the street lamps, took
out his handkerchief and wiped the sweat from his brow.
He had to sit there for a minute before his heartbeats
subsided and his hands steadied. It was not only reaction
to the hair-raising drive but a sense of exultation. Not only
had he overcome his phobia but he had proved himself
capable of handling a situation more demanding than any
race or rally driver was likely to face.

Then he felt for the wire in his pocket, went to the rear
and opened the cover of the engine. The 200 h.p. Fiat motor
was a stranger to him, but his racing and rally experience
had given him an instinct for an engine and the light from
the street lamp was strong enough for him to see what he
was doing. He traced the wires leading back to the ignition
switch and disconnected them, then used his own length
of wire to connect the terminal on the coil to the non-earth

terminal on the battery. He had already pulled the choke button out on the dashboard, so when he pressed the direct contact switch on the starter motor the engine fired. He closed the engine cover quickly, got back into the seat and adjusted the choke before the engine could stall.

Now he had transport, and a good chance of reaching Turin airport before the coach was even missed.

The hands of his watch under the brash light of the street lamp showed 1.27. A telephone call had established that there was a night flight to London at 3.30 a.m., and the Alitalia office had accepted the booking. Ken reckoned that if Ponti had put a tap on the line from the hotel he would have been stopped before now. So he had two hours to cover the hundred-odd miles to Caselle Airport, plant the coach, collect his ticket and get through emigration.

He depressed the clutch and for the first time engaged a gear. The coach jerked as he let the pedal up a bit too sharply and the engine nearly stalled. But he saved it in time and accelerated to warm her up. With the engine running and power assistance on both steering and brakes the coach was smooth and obedient, rather like a thorough-bred horse which has failed in its attempt to throw the rider and now acknowledges his power to control.

The road as far as Varese was hilly and sinuous and he could not reach any high speed. But from Varese he was on *autostrada* for twenty miles and able to cruise at between eighty and ninety. The coach was travelling so happily at this high speed that he decided to accept the longer route and go by *autostrada* all the way. It meant covering two sides of the triangle and going back almost as far as Milan but it reduced the likelihood of losing his way in some deserted town or being held up by a crawling juggernaut.

As he negotiated the complicated interchanges linking the motorways, it was already two o'clock. The signs for Turin showed that he had still a distance of 132 kilometres to cover, say eighty miles.

The speeding coach held a steady 80 m.p.h. along the

motorway and he silently thanked Joe for maintaining his engine in such tip-top condition. By five past three the lights of Turin were ahead and he was slowing to pick up signs pointing towards the airport to the north of the city.

It was here that he ran into difficulty and had to go right into the heart of the city to pick up a sign marked airport. In the end he had ten minutes to spare after parking the coach and immobilizing the engine.

As he walked across the main hall of the airport to the Alitalia desk he deliberately checked his pace, searching with his eyes the almost empty area. If the disappearance of the coach had been noticed the police might have put a watch on every airport.

But the girl to whom he gave his name showed no surprise and was unruffled by the fact that he had cut things so fine.

'Yes, Mr Fourseat, we have your ticket,' she said in English, handing him the usual folder. 'Will you pass immediately please to gate number 4?'

He was awakened by the popping of his ears as the Boeing made its descent to London Airport. It was still dark beyond the windows of the half empty aircraft. The time was 5.40.

'You have no luggage, sir?' a young Customs man said with polite disbelief as Ken passed through the room where the other passengers were claiming their suitcases.

'I wish I had. My suitcase was stolen from the foyer of my hotel in Turin just as I was leaving.'

'Oh, jolly bad luck.'

Fortunately the Renta people ran a twenty-four-hour service. The sleepy girl at the enquiry desk summoned up a smile for him when he enquired about a car, and showed him a list of the models available.

'I want something fast. Which is your best car?'

'The Rover V8 is our fastest, sir, but it's also one of the most expensive.'

'I'll take the Rover. It's only for one day.'

The elaborate form took time to fill in. Ken forced himself to check his impatience. He showed his driving licence and his credit card. Sleepiness had slowed the girl down, but she knew that if she made a mistake it could prove very expensive.

Before the documentation was complete a service driver in red overalls had come to the desk and when Ken had signed the form he led him out to the Rover. It was a very new scarlet model with automatic gear-box. The driver made sure that Ken understood the controls and enumerated the dials and switches for him.

'Are you all right, sir?' he asked anxiously, as he closed the driver's door. The customer had gone dead pale and was visibly sweating. His hands were clenched in his lap, making no move towards the controls.

'Yes.' The customer got the word out with difficulty. 'I'm quite all right.'

He seemed to make a great effort of will, then slowly his hand moved to the ignition key. The engine started with a roar. He relaxed, breathed deeply and turned to the driver with a smile.

'Okay. You see? Now, can you tell me the quickest route to Gatwick?'

'Gatwick? You go out the tunnel and there's signs all the way. No problem. You should be there in an hour easy.'

No problem. The words echoed in Ken's mind as the silky-smooth V8 took him through the long tunnel out of London Airport. It was wonderful to be again at the wheel of a powerful car. So far it was green lights all the way and he was becoming more and more confident that he had made the right decision. He would be at Gatwick around 7.15, before the unwilling guests of the Hotel Castelvecchio were even stirring for breakfast.

He parked the Rover at the main entrance to the Airport Main Hall despite the double yellow line and a warning notice that this was a no-waiting area. A few other cars were halted, setting down or picking up passengers.

'You're not going to leave it there, sir?'

The traffic warden on duty had moved over to intercept him before he went through the swing doors.

'I'll only be a minute,' Ken told him. 'Just have to pick up a suitcase.'

The Main Hall was comparatively quiet at this hour of the morning, although the loudspeaker was still faithfully relaying banal announcements. Piles of newspapers were being delivered to the magazine stand. A team of cleaners who had been going over the whole area were wheeling away the piles of litter they had swept up. The night-duty staff were looking at their watches and hoping that their reliefs would turn up on time.

Ken made a quick tour of the Main Hall, looking for a likely site for a wallful of luggage lockers. He did not want to ask for the information. He drew blank at ground level. Then he noticed that a party with their suitcases were heading for the staircase leading down past the toilets to the coach pick-up point.

He followed them down on the moving staircase and paused to let them get ahead. To his left the door marked Chaplain's Office was slightly open.

Against the grey concrete wall on the other side of the bleak space half a dozen telephone booths had been installed. Beside them stood the bank of Sablok Individual Luggage Lockers. Thirty-six rectangular metal coffers fixed to the concrete wall, with their doors facing outwards.

He felt in his pocket for the key, checking that there was no one in the telephone booths, waited until a group of passengers coming up from the bus station had passed out of sight.

It was easy to locate number 28. He inserted the key in the lock. It turned with a click. He swung the door open. Inside reposed a strong-looking suitcase, about two and a half feet in length. He reached in and pulled it out. The door swung to with its own weight and he made no attempt to withdraw the key.

The suitcase was heavy. He took a firm grip on it and made for the moving staircase.

At that moment the door of the chaplain's office was opened sharply. From it emerged a man with the build of a welter-weight boxer and fair hair cut to a military length.

'Just one moment, sir.'

Ken checked, realizing that the man was moving fast enough to cut him off if he made a run for it. A glance towards the stairs leading on down to the bus station showed him that another younger man was closing on him from that direction.

'What's the matter?'

'Police. Would you be so kind as to step into this office for a moment, sir?'

'I'd be glad to,' Ken said with relief. He was bewildered by this unexpected turn of events but reassured himself that what he had intended to do all along was make contact with the police in charge of the case.

The two plainclothes officers shepherded him closely as he went to the door of the chaplain's office. There was a kind of triumph about them as if a long wait had at last been rewarded. The younger man closed the door without turning his back on Ken.

His senior colleague had moved to the table in the middle of the room and pulled the telephone towards him. He dialled a number and was answered almost immediately.

'Duty sergeant? Spurling here. Tell the superintendent we have a customer. We're holding him in the chaplain's office at the airport. Right?'

He waited only long enough for the acknowledgement, then replaced the receiver.

'All right,' Ken said. 'What all this about?'

'Detective-Sergeant Spurling,' the man said, flashing his police card at Ken. The younger detective, whose face was pocked with the marks of boyhood acne, had closed up behind him. 'I wonder if you would be so kind as to open that suitcase.'

Ken had intended to examine the contents of the suitcase in privacy as soon as he was clear of the airport. But now that he thought about it there might be some advantage in having witnesses present when he did so. Especially if those witnesses were police officers, and the contents were likely to be material evidence in a murder trial.

He put the suitcase on the very untidy desk and pressed the catches to open it.

'It's locked.'

'And you don't have the keys?' The tone of the question indicated that the detective-sergeant expected a negative answer.

'No. It's not my suitcase, you see.'

Spurling nodded. He seemed in no way surprised by the statement.

'Then we'd better force it, don't you agree, sir?'

'If you have anything to force it with.'

'As it happens, I have.'

Spurling opened a drawer of the desk and took out a hefty claw hammer. He inserted the claw under a catch, applied leverage and forced it open. He did the same to the other side, then twisted the suitcase towards Ken.

'You open it, sir.'

Knowing that he was about to find the answer to the questions of the past week, Ken opened the lid as gingerly as if it was booby-trapped.

'I suggest you unpack it,' Spurling said quietly.

The top layer consisted of four men's shirts, still in their Cellophane laundry wrapping. Ken removed them and put them on the desk beside the suitcase.

The next layer was more puzzling. It consisted of semi-transparent women's nightdresses, sheath gowns of material like nylon, tights, brassieres and panties – all either unused or freshly laundered.

'Let's have those out, shall we?'

Intrigued and puzzled, Ken lifted the garments out and laid them on top of the others.

'That seems to be all.' He glanced round at the detective-constable in disappointment.

'May I look, sir?'

Spurling examined the edges of the suitcase and gave the bottom a tap.

'I believe there's a tray, sir. It lifts out.'

'You lift it out, Officer.'

'You have no objection, sir?'

'None at all.'

Spurling gripped the edges of the tray which fitted neatly into the suitcase providing a platform which prevented the garments at the bottom from being crushed. He pulled it out and placed it carefully on top of the pile of clothes.

Ken was staring at what was revealed in the lower compartment. Carefully inserted in plastic bags to protect them were three women's wigs – one long and blonde, one dark and curly, and one red-head. Alongside them lay a selection of corsets and suspender belts, all of them showing signs of having been worn at some time. Spurling removed the garments and wigs, holding them gingerly between finger and thumb. Beneath were revealed half a dozen illustrations torn from pornographic magazines and a wad of postcards depicting the extremer forms of sexual deviation. There was a black, shiny face-mask and hood and some kind of leather harness with heavy metal studs and buckles. Along the side of the case lay an obviously homemade cat-o'-nine-tails. In the corner was a neat coil of blue nylon rope. Ken knew at once that he had seen the replica of it on the night he and Diana had found Benson trussed up in his room.

Spurling lifted the cat-o'-nine-tails out. He raised his eyes to his colleague standing behind Ken's chair and nodded.

'Good God!' Ken was staring into the suitcase, struggling to sort out the implications of what he saw. In different

circumstances the queer collection of devices would have
been almost comic.

'Right. I think that's enough.' Spurling had straightened
up. Ken sensed the change of mood which had affected the
two men.

'Do you realize what this means?' he began. 'Christ, I've
been a bloody fool!'

'Before you say any more, sir, I have to caution you –'
'*What?*'

'I am arresting you on suspicion of murder. You will be
taken to the police station and charged.'

CHAPTER VIII

KEN CHECKED his mirror and on the brief stretch of de-restricted road accelerated to 120 m.p.h. The risk of being stopped for speeding weighed less with him than the urgency of getting back to Heathrow before the police net closed. Even in restricted zones he was travelling at speeds in excess of 60 or 70 m.p.h., watching his mirrors, calculating the moves of other drivers on the road, keeping a weather eye open for the vans the police use for radar traps. He was exploiting the car's potential to the full, holding the lower gears to get maximum acceleration from traffic lights, relying on his Girling discs to stop him in an emergency. Normally a considerate driver, he was for once disregarding the rules, blasting pogglers with his horns, passing on the wrong side when necessary, using engine power and the leech-like qualities of the tyres to jink from one traffic lane to another.

Now that he had time to think about it he realized how the police had come to connect locker number 28 with the murders of Mrs Rayburn and the crime in the Crown Hotel. The fingerprint experts must have checked the prints found in the chaplain's office with those left by the killer of Tony Draper. They were meticulous enough to have gone over the whole area around the chaplains' hide-out and must have found matching prints on the Sablok locker. A natural reaction by the superintendent in charge would be to put observations on the locker, using the office as a look-out, and patiently wait for the fly to walk into the net.

Of course he could have established his innocence by giving his own fingerprints. But having caught him in possession of the suitcase the police would not have released him without prolonged questioning and verification. And his dash from Castelvecchio could hardly have ingratiated him with the Italian police. Even on reflection he did not regret making the break from Spurling, though his action must have been interpreted as a confession of guilt. He simply had to get back to Castelvecchio and Diana. He checked his mirror again and as he entered a 40-m.p.h. zone reduced his speed to 80.

To his relief there was no queue in front of the Alitalia desk at London Airport.

'Can you tell me when your next flight to Turin is, please?'

A glance round the hall in Terminal Building Number Two. No evidence that a cordon of plainclothes men was closing in on him. The Rover was on the fourth floor of the multi-storey car park, nestling between a Bentley and a Jaguar. It was goodbye to the deposit but that was a detail.

'We have a flight to Turin at 2.15, sir. Shall I book you on that?'

'What about Milan?'

'There's a flight to Milan at 11.40. It's pretty booked up but we might have a single.'

Eight forty-seven now. A wait of three hours was unthinkable.

'What's your next flight to any point in Europe?'

'*Any* point?' She stared at him in surprise.

'Well, Geneva, Rome, Paris. That sort of thing.'

'We have a flight to Zürich at nine o'clock which is not fully booked, but it's already been called. I doubt if you can catch it.'

'Give me the ticket and I'll have a try. I'll bring it back and have it changed if I miss it.'

She raised her eyebrows, and began reluctantly to make out the ticket. He tried to think of some explanation that would make his haste seem less suspicious.

'I'll hire a car at Zürich,' he told her. 'That'll get me to Varese almost as quickly. It's somebody's wedding, you see.'

'You've left it a bit late, haven't you?' was her only

comment as she handed him the ticket and verified the
number on his credit card.

Even with the powerful engine of an Opel Ascona 81 under
the bonnet he had to drop to second gear to attack the
steep hill leading up from the lake to Castelvecchio.

It was just coming up to three o'clock. He had done well
to average fifty miles an hour from Zürich over roads
which had offered spectacular mountain views but made
any real speed impossible. Too impatient to wait for the
next train through the tunnel, he had decided to drive over
the top of the 6000-foot St Gotthard Pass. It had been a
thrilling drive and he had revelled in the fantastic cornering
of the rally-bred Ascona, with its limited slip differential
and wide Goodyear Grand Prix tyres. But by the time
he hit the comparatively fast stretch along the valley to
Bellinzona, his hands were blistered from friction on the
steering wheel and constant gear changes.

He throttled back when he rounded a corner and saw
above him the silhouette of the hotel, with its characteristic
Ghibelline battlements crowning the eastern tower. He knew
that he had to quell this sense of urgency in him, slow down
his tempo, think and act coolly. He had been gone a mere
fourteen hours but so much could have happened in that
time.

He stopped the car on the main road outside the rear
entrance through which he had coaxed the coach the
previous night, locked it and went up the back avenue on
foot.

From the cover of the cypress trees he scanned the
gardens at the back of the house. There was no sign of any
carabinieri patrol. He walked quickly across the gardens,
reached the wall of the hotel and moved along it till he
found a back door outside which were piled discarded fruit
boxes, and plastic sacks of refuse. The passage beyond was
deserted. It led through to the main hall. The kitchen staff
had gone off duty and were enjoying a siesta. He could hear

voices near the front door but there was no problem about reaching the lift without being seen.

He took it up to the floor Diana's room was on, checked that there was no one in the corridor before stepping out. He tried the handle of her room before knocking. To his surprise it opened. He went in, closing it behind him.

Of Diana there was no sign. Not only she but her luggage and all the clothes which had been lying around were gone. Even the bed had been made up with clean sheets.

Diana had hardly slept that night after she had watched Ken's dimly outlined shape flit across the garden. In the first place she was sure that about an hour after he had gone someone tried the door of her room. She got up and wedged an upright chair under the handle in the way her former husband had once shown her. After that sleep just would not come. She was tormented by a conviction that Ken had made the wrong decision and would only run into some terrible trouble. But once he had taken it into his head to do something it was impossible to reason with him. Yet this very impetuosity was part of the character which had so quickly come to dominate her thoughts. When she prayed for his safety it was with passionate sincerity.

It was about nine, when most people were breakfasting, that a commotion outside indicated that the disappearance of the coach had been spotted. The *carabinieri*, realizing that they had boobed, invaded the hotel with guns at the ready and made all the guests assemble for a check.

Of course, Ken's absence was noted.

In the ensuing excitement, the *carabinieri* had little sympathy for the Prestons' complaint that a night prowler had tried to get into the room where Emma and Nigel were sleeping.

At a few minutes after ten Ponti drove up in his Fiat, white with anger. He fired questions at every member of the party. No one admitted to knowing anything about Ken's movements.

'And you, signora.' He glared at Diana, trying to brow-beat her into some sort of confession. 'You know nothing about the movements of your friend?'

'No. Nothing.'

'Well, at least we know who our criminal is. This is an admission of guilt.'

He stormed off, presumably to put out a general call for the Fiat coach and its occupant.

The morning crawled by. Lunch-time came and as the guests assembled in the dining-room they saw that Gabriella was accompanied by a young man with a fair moustache, horn-rimmed spectacles and an English club tie.

He called for silence and announced himself as a member of the British Consulate staff.

'I am sorry that it has taken us so long to sort your problem out, ladies and gentlemen, but I'm glad to say that at last we can see daylight. In view of the defection of Mr Forsythe the police do not feel they need detain you any longer, so you will be free to leave this afternoon.'

A general buzz of relief broke out and the young man had to raise his hand again.

'There's one exception, I'm afraid. Mrs Meredith, I'm sorry to say that the police have insisted on detaining you. When the party moves on you will be transferred to a hotel in Varese.'

'Does that mean I'm being arrested?' Diana enquired, very white in the face.

'Not officially arrested. A kind of house arrest, as I understand it. You can rest assured that we will see you get proper legal advice.'

Condemned without trial, Diana thought bitterly, at least by my fellow passengers. As they filtered out from the dining-room and went off to pack their bags everyone studiously avoided her, as if she had ceased to exist or was suffering from bubonic plague.

Only Benson showed any sympathy. He hung back as the others gradually left the dining-room empty.

'I say, I am sorry about this. Fancy suspecting you. I wish there was something I could do to help.'

'Thanks.' Diana looked at him gratefully. 'I don't think there is. I'd better go and pack my things. Ponti is sending a car to collect me this afternoon.'

But when she had packed her suitcases and seen them taken down to the hall she had second thoughts. If she was going to be left entirely alone here perhaps somebody ought to be told why Ken had decided to go back to Gatwick. And he had said that if she was in deep trouble the one person she could trust was Benson.

She went down to find out the number of his room and saw him standing out in the sunlight at the front of the hotel.

'Mr Benson, you offered to help me just now if you could.'

He started, as if a deep reverie had been interrupted, then quickly put on his paternal smile.

'Yes. If there's anything I can do.'

'Can we go somewhere we won't be overheard?'

Carabinieri were on duty at both the front and back entrances now and she knew that as soon as the others departed in the coach which had been ordered she would be under closer guard.

'What about this path?' Benson proposed. 'It leads to a rather attractive spinney. I know because I was there this morning.'

They walked slowly till they were in the shade of the trees bordering the path. Benson's manner was very protective, almost proprietorial.

'I want someone to know why Ken went away,' she blurted out, breaking the barrier of silence with an effort. 'It was not a confession of guilt, as Ponti thinks.'

'Oh? Why did he go then?'

'He wanted to get some evidence and he knew he could find it back at Gatwick.'

Benson had stopped but he did not turn towards her.

'What sort of evidence?'

'He didn't know exactly. Something that would explain all these attacks and apparent thefts.'

Benson was still staring ahead down the path.

'What made him think he would find such evidence at Gatwick?'

Diana hesitated. Up till now nobody but she and Ken had known about the key. But for Ken's sake it was important that someone else should realize that he'd had a genuine reason for eluding the Italian police.

'He had a key. We thought it was the key of one of those personal lockers for luggage at Gatwick. Now, when you get back to England could you find out who the police officer in charge of the investigation is and tell him this? In case something has happened to Ken, it was locker number 28.'

She glanced round at his face. His mouth was twitching and there was a peculiar fixity about his stare.

'How did this key come into his possession?'

'It all goes back to that night at Gatwick.' Diana scanned the path ahead, trying to make out what could have so riveted his attention. Despite his questions she wondered if he was really concentrating on what she was telling him. 'Mrs Rayburn apparently found this key in the sort of holdall she had. She asked me if I'd hand it in to the Lost Property Office and I said I would. But what with the rush of our flight being called I simply forgot. I gave it to Ken in Venice and he promised to remember to hand it in when we got back to Gatwick.'

Benson took off his spectacles, wiped them with a handkerchief and put them back on again. It was done clumsily as if all his fingers had become thumbs.

'Let's move on a bit.' He shot a look back down the path. 'I can't bear the thought that those bad-tempered *carabinieri* might be watching us.'

Sunlight filtered through the leaves of the trees, turning the pathway into a dappled tunnel. It was very quiet and since midday the air had become heavy. Even the small animals and birds who usually rustle or sing in such places seemed to be having their siesta. The twigs crackled under their feet as they walked, crisply audible in the stillness.

Benson remained absolutely silent till they had rounded a bend in the path. Then he stopped again and this time he let her see his face.

'This is a very difficult situation,' he said, so softly that he might have been talking to himself.

She wondered why her statement had brought about such a change in him. His usually pink, smooth cheeks had gone grey. His eyes behind the round spectacles had retreated further into their sockets. He had thrust his hands into his pockets to hide their trembling. She wondered whether he was subject to sudden heart attacks.

'Mr Benson. Are you feeling all right?'

He said: 'I feel most peculiar. I think I may be going to faint.'

She saw him sway, moved forward to support him. At that moment a voice called out: 'Hold it!'

She spun round, saw Ken walking quickly towards them down the path.

'Ken! So you got back! How did you –'

'I'll tell you all about it later, Diana.' He brushed her greeting and questions aside. He was very controlled and very watchful. His eyes had never left Benson. 'Would you please go back to the hotel and wait there? I'll join you when I've had a talk with Benson.'

'Actually, I've just been telling Mr Benson –'

'Diana, do as I ask, please!'

It was a tone of voice she had not heard before. She studied each of their faces, saw that there was something here which she did not understand, something frightening and disturbing. She nodded and started back towards the hotel. Before she turned the bend in the path she could not resist a quick glance back. Her last picture of Benson was of him standing in the same attitude, just waiting and staring at Ken with a haunted, hypnotized expression.

Ken waited till she was out of sight before he spoke. He felt no sense of triumph and certainly none of danger. Now that he was facing the man, knowing the kind of act of which he was capable he could only experience utter revulsion. He thought his expression must be very like that of Detective-Sergeant Spurling when the suitcase had been emptied.

'Yes,' he said. 'I know. I have been back to Gatwick and seen what was in your suitcase.'

Benson's mouth was quivering. Unable to bear the accusation in Ken's eyes, he had turned his head away.

'What's so incredible is that you had to carry all that transvestite gear around with you and at least two pieces of evidence that connected you with the murder of Tony Draper. What possessed you to do that? Were they souvenirs of your happiest moments that you couldn't bear to part with?'

Benson's spectacles were misting over. He reached up, took them off and thrust them into one of his baggy jacket pockets.

'Of course,' Ken continued remorselessly, 'you could feel pretty safe about bringing the stuff to Italy. The Customs never search the luggage of tourists coming *into* the country. And I don't suppose you would ever have gone back. The package tour was a way of getting out of England inconspicuously.' Benson did not answer. He was staring at the back of his right hand, perhaps admiring that excessively long little-finger nail.

'You must have been thrown into a fair old panic at Gatwick when the police check began. You thought they were looking for you. So you hit on the idea of hiding the case in the Sablok locker, and when the detective came to question us all you dropped the key into Mrs Rayburn's holdall. You found her alone while we were all at dinner and somehow lured her down to the chaplain's office. Then when you tried to get it back you found she hadn't got it.

So what was the point of killing her? Is that how you get your kicks?'

Ken's tone had hardened. He could feel the anger in him coming out. He had hardly eaten for eighteen hours and was aching with fatigue. Now he found an almost sadistic satisfaction in flailing Benson with the truth.

'So the tour which was planned to be such a cosy way of escaping from the country turned into a desperate race to save your skin. You had to find that key before the tour ended and you had to dispose of anyone who might have noticed that you had gone down to the toilet *with* your suitcase and come back *without* it.'

Benson chanced a sly look at Ken's face. He had no difficulty in focusing without his glasses, but his eyes had a look of indecent nakedness.

'You seem to forget that I was attacked myself.'

'Cleverly faked. You made a mess of your room, put the gag in your own mouth and tied your own ankles. You could have got your wrists into a rope round your waist and pulled the slip-knot by using the door-knob or something. They tell me that there are people who enjoy that sort of thing. And you're kinked enough to have inflicted that head wound on yourself.'

Benson put a hand up to feel the patch of plaster which still covered the cut on his temple.

'Where is the suitcase now?' His voice was scarcely audible.

'The police have got it. Your collection of transvestite gear, the sticking plaster you used to gag that wretched fellow, the cat-o'-nine-tails made no doubt by your own fair hands –'

'That's enough!' Benson cut in, his voice almost cracking into a hysterical falsetto.

'You're going to have to face it in the end, you know,' Ken said more quietly. 'I know perverts are two a penny these days but you seem to have just about every deviation in the book. Plus a pathological urge to kill.'

'I didn't mean to kill him. I'd only intended to punish him. Then when I saw him lying there like that – Everything went red and I can't remember what happened. I swear I can't remember killing him.'

'Very convenient.' Ken studied the man with curiosity, trying to imagine how he must look when the lust to kill took possession of him. Perhaps he did it with the same expression as he had on his face now – mouth slack and wet, eyes oddly filmed, hands clenching and unclenching, sweat on his brow and with it all a touch of petulant self-justification.

'But you can remember killing Mrs Rayburn –'

'That was different. I admit I had to use some force but it was some kind of heart attack that really killed her.'

'Then what about Alice Norman and Gareth Jones? That was deliberate enough, wasn't it? And the night when you slashed me with your knife in Diana Meredith's room –'

'Nobody had a right!' Benson's lower lip was quivering. He was like a child about to give way to a storm of weeping. 'You may not realize it but I am very respected in my field. Nobody had a right to pry into my things! That's my own world, my own secret world! No one has a right to expose it.'

It was only then that Ken thought he understood Benson's motive. He had a sense of shame so strong that it urged him on to seek out and kill rather than allow the twisted pervert behind the respectable façade to be exposed. Such exposure was beyond endurance and Ken was watching the consequences of it now. The Benson whom the world knew had dissolved, leaving behind a cowering energumen, a snail dragged from its shell by the bird which has cracked it on a stone.

'I suppose,' Ken said in a tone of wonder, 'they'll plead insanity. And, by God, I think they're right. But if you really are a split personality, as you seem to claim, I'm afraid you are both going to have to stand in the dock and face it. Your secret world is liable to become very public.'

'Never!' Benson shook his head with a strange conviction. 'Do you think I have not made provision for this possibility?'

He slumped down on the seat at the side of the path, groping in his pocket for his inhaler.

'In a way it's a relief that I don't have to pretend any longer, as if a great responsibility had been taken away from me. You see, you've got it all wrong. You just have no idea what it is like to be me. No idea. I'd like to try and explain, but I don't think we'd be left in peace for long enough.'

'If you want to talk,' Ken said with a sense of compassion which surprised him, 'go ahead and do so. I'm not the police. I won't take it down in writing.'

Benson had screwed the case off the inhaler and shaken a small capsule into the palm of his hand. He had not really been listening to what Ken said. He looked up at the younger man with a half smile. His face was shiny pale and his eyes were not focused.

'The prisoner's release,' he said and raised the palm of his hand to his mouth.

Too late Ken understood what was happening and threw himself forward. Even as he made his lunge Benson's teeth bit on the capsule. The result was virtually instantaneous. His body was limp as Ken cannoned into it. The force of his rush carried both men off the seat, down on to the patch of grass and wild flowers beside it. A faint nutty tang mingled with the scent of crushed petals.

Ken disentangled himself from Benson's arms and legs and stood up. The convulsions had begun and the body was jerking as if it was being subjected to torture by electric shock. But Benson's eyes were half closed, the pupils had rolled upwards and his mind was well beyond consciousness of the contortions of his body.

'Too easy,' Ken muttered. 'Too bloody easy.'

He began to run back towards the château. There might still be time to pump some sort of antidote into Benson, to bring him back to face the judgement he richly deserved. He was moving at full speed when he rounded the bend in the path and collided violently with a dark-suited man who was coming equally fast in the opposite direction.

As he recovered his balance Ken saw that it was Detective-Sergeant Spurling. Behind him, outpaced in the sprint by twenty yards, trotted a breathless Inspector Ponti.

'No,' Spurling agreed, 'I can't say we were very pleased when we found that you'd turned the table on us and locked us in the chaplain's office. But when the kerfuffle had died down we decided to check the fingerprints you'd left on the suitcase with those the murderer had left at the Crown Hotel and on the steel locker of the office. We realized then that we'd got the wrong man.'

'How did you know I'd come back here?'

Ken was sitting with Spurling in the very office where Ponti had put Diana through such a tough interrogation. The British detective, realizing that his case was solved, had left it to the Italian police to deal with the body of Benson.

'It wasn't hard to work out. I had a special jet fly me to Milan, but frankly I didn't think you'd be able to get here so quickly. You beat me by ten minutes. I was just in time to meet a very alarmed Mrs Meredith coming into the hotel.'

'I'm sorry about my rather violent reactions at Gatwick, Inspector –'

'Detective-Sergeant, sir. And likely to remain so after the way I let you pull the wool over our eyes.'

'Then I'm even more sorry. Will there be charges to answer when I get back to England?'

'Well, sir,' Spurling said, with slow relish, 'you were timed through a speed trap at –'

The CID man's pleasure at keeping Ken in suspense was thwarted by the arrival of Inspector Ponti, accompanied by a police doctor who spoke remarkably good English.

'He's dead of course,' Spurling said, addressing his remark to the doctor.

'Oh yes. Hydrocyanic acid is a quick-acting poison when taken in that quantity.'

'Do you think that could be the same poison as killed the Norman girl?'

The doctor nodded and pursed his lips noncommittally.

'It could well be. A small dose can produce such symptoms, but as I was not in a position to –'

'What beats me,' Spurling interjected, 'is how he administered poison to the girl in a place like a public hotel.'

'You observed the long nail on the little finger?' Ponti said in slow but excellent English. Ken realized with anger that the whole charade about using an interpreter had been simply a device to throw his suspects off balance and give him more time to think up his next question. 'I investigated a case once in Tripoli where the principal guest was poisoned by his host at a crowded dinner-table. The mystery was baffling till we discovered that it is an old Arab trick to secrete poison in the nail of the little finger and to thrust it into the piece of food which you offer to your guest. Benson could have planted poison in a fruit or ice-cream which he was handing to the signorina.'

'I'll remember that one,' Spurling said. 'Could come in handy with my mother-in-law.'

Through the window of the office Ken had seen Diana walking thoughtfully out towards the terrace where the tour party had taken coffee. He remembered saying to her that no one in the group was quite what they seemed to be. The remark now seemed a monstrous understatement.

'Are we free to go now, Inspector?'

'Detective-Sergeant, sir,' Spurling corrected automatically. There was a glint of secret amusement in his eye. 'My Italian colleague is going to want you to answer a few questions, but before you make any statement I think I should warn you that anything you say –'